THE SPIDER:
REIGN OF THE SNAKE MEN

MASTER OF MEN!

THE SPIDER®

REIGN OF
THE SNAKE MEN

By Grant Stockbridge

STEEGER BOOKS • 2020

CHAPTER 1
THE MAN IN THE TOMBS

A T EXACTLY five minutes before three p.m. Eastern Standard Time, Richard Wentworth, *alias* the Spider, alighted from the taxicab at the Criminal Courts Building on Center Street. After the cab had departed, he stood for a moment looking up at the barred cell windows of the Tombs Prison, which was directly opposite, and connected to the Court House by the famous old Bridge of Sighs, that spanned Center Street.

Uniformed policemen and plain clothes detectives passed, actually brushing shoulders with him. But they failed to recognize the man whom they would have given a year's pay to capture. For a few deft touches of skillful make-up—the application of tufts of gray hair to the eyebrows and the temples, the insertion of cunningly contrived, thin contour plates into the nostrils, thus widening the entire nose—had so altered his appearance that he felt quite secure from detection, except for some unforeseen circumstance.

There seemed to be a good deal of excitement around the Criminal Courts Building, and at Police Headquarters, a short distance away. Officers hurried about with set, nervous faces, their hands always near their guns. Occasionally a squad car would roar past, its siren wide open, answering an emergency call; frequently, the disturbing clang of ambulance bells would

1

sound as the mercy cars sped through the streets on call. Wentworth had noticed the strange tension throughout the city all that day and the day before. There was something ominous, something of calamity in the air.

And now, things were happening—strange things that called for racing squad cars and clanging ambulances that went to widely scattered parts of the city. Yet the newspapers and the

The hooded men came on, never swerving,

like dreadful automatons mocking death.

radio were queerly silent on the subject, as if a tight police censorship had been clamped down on news. Whatever the cause of these emergency calls, it was something the police feared to reveal to the public.

Wentworth's face reflected nothing of the swift, troubled thoughts that raced through his mind. To all appearances he was an unconcerned sightseer inspecting the famed old Tombs Prison, which was a landmark of New York City. In reality, his gaze was fixed upon a certain barred window on the second floor. Behind those bars he could discern a white, gaunt face—a face that had once been ruddy and full of life and health, but which was now tinged by prison pallor.

The Spider's throat constricted in quick sympathy. That man, wrecked in health and in spirit, who looked out so hopelessly from behind the bars, was Wentworth's good friend, Stanley Kirkpatrick, former police commissioner, now disgraced, awaiting trial on a charge of murder.

Time was when Richard Wentworth could have come down here to Police Headquarters, could have walked boldly into his friend's office, and asked what was happening in the city that called for police squad cars and ambulances. But today a stranger sat in Kirkpatrick's office, and Wentworth dared not show himself in his true identity. For Richard Wentworth had also been framed for murder by the same enemy who had framed the police commissioner. But Wentworth had been fortunate enough to evade capture, had fought a grim battle without quarter against that common enemy.

In the end, Wentworth had triumphed, but at a high price.

Tang-akhmut, the mysterious Man from the East, who called himself the Living Pharaoh, had been driven from the city, despoiled of the power he had usurped. But with his disappearance had gone the last chance of clearing Kirkpatrick and Wentworth of the spurious murder charge.

Wentworth had inaugurated cautious inquiries with a view to finding Tang-akhmut or his beautiful, dangerous sister, the Princess Issoris. For only through them could he establish the innocence of himself and his friend. Those inquiries had ended in a blank wall. There was no trace of the Man from the East.

So the Spider was now thrusting his head into the jaws of peril to rescue Kirkpatrick from the barred cell up there in the Tombs. His plans had been perfected carefully, and he had today taken advantage of the break in luck that he had waited for patiently. Through a fortunate chance, he was enabled to make a bold effort at rescue. The success or failure of the effort would be apparent in a few minutes.

TEARING HIS eyes from the face of his friend, Richard Wentworth, *alias* the Spider, turned, and boldly entered the wide doorway of the Criminal Courts Building.

He ascended in the elevator to the third floor, passing on the way half a dozen headquarters detectives whom he knew to be assigned to the hunt for himself. None of them gave him a second glance. It was farthest from their thoughts that the man for whom they were searching far and wide should present himself brazenly in their very midst.

On the third floor, Wentworth unhesitatingly entered the office marked: "District Attorney, County of New York."

5

A secretary glanced up at him inquiringly, and he said: "I should like to see Mr. Lingwell, the District Attorney, please."

"Is Mr. Lingwell expecting you?"

"Yes. We have an appointment at five, but I'm a bit early. You may tell him that Mr. Woods of Washington is calling."

The girl smiled quickly. "Oh yes, Mr. Woods. You can go right in. Mr. Lingwell's office is the last room on the right."

Wentworth passed through the low wooden gate, and down along the corridor flanked on both sides by the cubbyholes of innumerable assistant district attorneys, until he reached Samuel Lingwell's office.

The district attorney arose from behind his desk as the Spider entered. He was a short man, rather inclined to corpulence, with a totally bald head and very large ears that stood out almost at right angles from his skull. He shook hands eagerly with Wentworth, indicated a chair. "I'm damned glad you've come, Woods. The situation here is getting a bit out of hand. I hadn't expected you till later."

"I got an earlier train out of Washington, and I thought I might just as well come right up."

"Good, good!" Lingwell rubbed his hands. "By the way—just as a formality, of course—you have some—er—identification? No offense, you know—"

Wentworth raised a hand, smiling. "Not at all, Mr. Lingwell.

6

It's the proper thing. Here you are." He produced a small wallet, flipped it open to a card bearing a small likeness of himself just as he appeared now, with the graying temples and the bushy eyebrows. Across the card and the photograph was his signature: "Walter A. Woods." And the card read:

UNITED STATES OF AMERICA
DEPARTMENT OF JUSTICE

At the bottom of the card was the facsimile signature of the director of the Federal Bureau of Investigation. Lingwell could not know that the card was a clever forgery, finished not a half hour ago by a printer and engraver who were deeply in the Spider's debt. The ink had been quickly dried by a special process, and the card had been then sprinkled lightly with a mixture of water and salt, to cover up its freshness. Also, Lingwell could not know that the true Mr. Woods of Washington was even then on the train, speeding toward New York.

Lingwell could not know that last night, when he had phoned Washington from his home and asked for a special agent, his Chinese house man had overheard that conversation. The Chinese had promptly developed a severe case of stomach ache, and had received permission to take the evening off and go to a doctor. The stomach ache had disappeared no sooner than the house man left the district attorney's home. He had gone, not to a doctor, but to the heart of Chinatown where the head of his tong, one Yang Chung by name, listened carefully to his report, thanked him gravely, and dismissed him.

Yang Chung, a Chinese gun runner, had allied himself with

Wentworth in the struggle against Tang-akhmut. And their friendship had grown as a result of the alliance. So the shrewd yellow gun runner had at once phoned Wentworth.

ALL THIS, Lingwell could not know. Therefore he cast only a cursory glance at the card of identification, and plunged at once into his story. "I'll admit I'm licked, Woods. The city is up against something too big for us. You know the trouble we've had here in the past few months. Tang-akhmut demoralized the police force, and almost got control of the town—"

"I've heard," Wentworth drawled, "that it was the Spider who drove him out."

"The Spider? No, no. Richard Wentworth did it. Wentworth and Kirkpatrick are both charged with murder. Wentworth had some sort of private feud with Tang-akhmut, and the two fought it out. But now we're looking for Wentworth. He's a fugitive from justice!"

Richard Wentworth nodded, veiling his eyes. Lingwell, like the rest of the public, did not know that Wentworth and the dreaded Spider were one and the same. Even Kirkpatrick, Wentworth's very close friend, did not know it for sure. He perhaps suspected the truth, but he had never been able to prove it.

That was good. As long as Wentworth kept the identity of the Spider veiled in mystery, he could operate with more or less impunity. The Spider was hated by the police, and feared by the underworld. Long ago, Richard Wentworth had created that dreaded personality, under the cloak of which he waged relentless war on the underworld. It was in that capacity that he had battled Tang-akhmut. But the sinister Man from the East had discovered what even the police could not prove; namely, that Wentworth was the Spider. It was for that reason that the so-called Living Pharaoh had framed Wentworth and Kirkpatrick.

The Spider jerked back to Lingwell as he heard the district attorney say: "But let's not bother about Wentworth now. He'll be caught eventually. Sooner or later he'll try to rescue his friend Kirkpatrick from the Tombs, and then we'll spring a neat little trap we've ringed up here. But now, there's something far more serious. Woods—" he leaned over the desk, and dropped his voice—*"I'm afraid that Tangakhmut is back!"*

Wentworth snapped into instant startled attention. So his instinct had been right again! That unaccountable feeling of brooding, impending peril which had obsessed him for the last two days had not been without foundation. With an effort he repressed the eager questions that rose to his lips. It would not do to betray himself to Lingwell now.

Forcing his voice to a tone of scoffing disbelief he said: "Tangakhmut? Don't be absurd, Lingwell. We had word in Washington that he and his sister, the Princess Issoris, had fled the country. What leads you to believe he's back?"

For answer Lingwell silently took from his desk a queer, brass plaque. It was circular in shape and about six inches in diameter. There was nothing on it except the figure of a coiled cobra, which had been stamped into the brass. The surface of the plaque itself was painted jet black, except for the figure of the cobra, so that the coiled reptile stood out in livid contrast to its black background. There was no lettering or inscription of any kind on the plaque.

Wentworth examined the strange object closely, then raised his eyes to see that Lingwell was watching him. "Since you've come from Washington," the District Attorney said, "you probably haven't seen that before. But in New York, it's become a common sight within the last few days. It appears in the windows of almost every store in town."

"A racket?" Wentworth asked softly.

Lingwell nodded. He swallowed, and licked dry lips with his tongue. "A racket, yes. But nothing like we've ever seen before, Woods!"

HIS PERSPIRING fingers gripped the Spider's wrist. "Did you hear the ambulances and the squad cars on your way down here? They were answering calls to stores where this plaque is not displayed. Dreadful things seem to happen—to stores that don't show this damn thing in the window. In one place today, a madman walked in and dropped a bomb on the counter, then ran out just in time to escape the explosion; in half a dozen other places, sticks of Greek fire were thrown into stores by half naked maniacs who didn't *seem* to care about their own lives. Not a single one of them was captured alive. And this afternoon—" Lingwell tapped an accompaniment to his next words with a pudgy forefinger on Wentworth's wrist—*"ninety—cases—of—typhoid—have—been—reported—in—the—city."*

Wentworth took a deep breath. "Those ninety cases—they were also in stores without plaques?"

"Yes. But that isn't all. We've known for a week that something was brewing. Fremont and Tynan— the biggest department store in the city—reported to us a week ago that they were approached with the proposition to install these plaques in their windows. They were told that it was a valuable protection—"

"Against what?" Wentworth asked.

Lingwell shrugged. "They weren't told. They refused to buy the plaques. And the next day Lawrence Fremont, the president of the concern disappeared. He hasn't been heard from since. Our stores on Fifth Avenue also report that they have been approached. In each case the emissary is a woman. The price she demands for the plaques is anywhere from five hundred to ten thousand dollars—depending upon the size of the store. Many have bought the plaques after hearing what happened at Fremont and Tynan's and at several other places that held out. The city is rapidly coming into the grip of the unknown organization that is selling those plaques. If Fremont and Tynan's, and a few of the other big ones, capitulate, it will mean that this sinister symbol of the cobra will rule the city!"

Lingwell pushed away from the desk and strode up and down in front of Wentworth. "We can't handle the situation, Woods. Frankly, a man like Kirkpatrick, at the head of the police department, might have been equal to it. But Kirkpatrick is in jail, and it is my duty to prosecute. I've taken it upon myself to call in you Department of Justice men. You've got to help!"

"You think," Wentworth said thoughtfully, "that anything done on such a scale must have a man like Tang-akhmut behind it?"

"That's what I'm afraid of, Woods. Will you help me?"

Wentworth pushed back his chair and got up. "I'll help you, Lingwell, on one condition!"

"Anything. Anything you require, Woods!"

"All right. The condition is that you send for Commissioner Kirkpatrick. Have him brought here from his cell for an interview."

Lingwell frowned. "Of course, as the District Attorney, I have the authority to have any prisoner brought here for questioning. But I don't see what he has to do—"

"That will become apparent to you later," Wentworth told him coldly. "Now please do as I say!"

Lingwell hesitated, then shrugged. "I confess it's beyond my depth. But if you insist, I'll do it."

Wentworth strove to hide the fierce joy in his eyes as Lingwell returned to his desk, pushed a button on the callophone, and gave instructions that Kirkpatrick be brought from the Tombs at once.

IN A few moments an attendant entered with a release order for Lingwell to sign. This was the usual form without which no prisoner is permitted to leave the Tombs. After the attendant had left, Lingwell explained to Wentworth that it would be about ten minutes before Kirkpatrick could be brought in.

"Perhaps you will explain to me, while we're waiting, why you want him—"

The Spider was saved the necessity of inventing an explanation by the sudden flaring of a green light on the signal board behind the District Attorney's desk. This signal board was hooked up with headquarters and indicated that an emergency message was being transmitted on the telautograph in the outer office. Almost at once, the telautograph operator entered with the transcript of the message, Lingwell read it and his pudgy face paled. Silently he handed the paper to Wentworth who scanned it quickly. The message read:

> Cablegram from Paris Sûreté advises us Tang-akhmut was last seen in Cayenne, French Guiana, aiding in escape of group of dangerous criminals from penal settlement there. Sûreté is broadcasting warning to police departments everywhere to be on lookout. They were reported to have made their way to the Leper Colony near Araguary River. But when government troops surrounded the spot the colony was found to have been burned to the ground. Further details will follow.

Wentworth's eyes narrowed, and his keenly analytical mind ran swiftly over the situation. Things that were transpiring in the city now had every earmark of having been engineered by Tang-akhmut. The Man from the East never indulged in half measures. Such a campaign of terrorization as Lingwell had described was characteristic of the Living Pharaoh.

It was entirely possible that the woman who had offered the hideous black plaques for sale was the Princess Issoris. And if

13

Tang-akhmut had aided the escape of desperate criminals from the French Penal Settlement, then he must have those criminals with him here in New York. It was important to discover how large a band of desperadoes the Man from the East had with him. With a large band he would have difficulty in finding a suitable headquarters in a city like New York, without being easily spotted.

And Wentworth knew from bitter experience in the past that the only way to checkmate Tang-akhmut was to carry the fight directly to his headquarters. Granting that Lingwell was right in his assumption that the Living Pharaoh had returned, then it became imperative to discover the enemy's headquarters.

His train of thought was interrupted by the entrance of a deputy warden and the prisoner, Commissioner Kirkpatrick.

Wentworth's blood chilled at sight of the thin, hollow-cheeked Kirkpatrick. Prison, together with its accompanying worries, had done the ex-commissioner no good. In place of his former crisp buoyancy and sharp efficiency, he now bore himself with a listless, lackadaisical air that bespoke a crushed and broken spirit. He looked at Wentworth and no hint of recognition lit up his weary, sunken eyes.

Lingwell said to him: "Kirkpatrick, this is Mr. Woods, a special agent of the Department of Justice. He wishes to interview you."

Kirkpatrick nodded drearily and took the seat that Lingwell indicated, while the deputy warden remained near the door.

The District Attorney motioned to Wentworth. "Go ahead, Mr. Woods. Ask your questions."

The Spider shook his head. "If you don't mind, I'd like to question the prisoner *in private.*" As he made this request, a certain subtle change had taken place in the inflection of his voice. It assumed a peculiar timbre which the voice of Mr. Woods had lacked up to now, but which was characteristic of Richard Wentworth.

AT THE sound of that familiar voice Kirkpatrick jerked upright out of his lethargic listlessness. His eyes focused in sudden hope upon Wentworth's face, and slowly the glad light of recognition flickered there. All the apathy fled from the prisoner's posture. His gaze met Wentworth's squarely, and the two old friends exchanged understanding glances. The Spider's heart waned. This was like old times again when these two had trod perilous paths together, the lives of both depending upon the mental alertness of each.

Kirkpatrick understood that Wentworth was here to effect his rescue, and he sat now taut, all his lassitude gone, transformed in a moment from a weary prisoner into the man of action that he had always been. Though he did not know what Wentworth's plan might be, he was ready for his cue.

Lingwell was saying: "But look here, Mr. Woods, that's highly irregular. I don't see why it's necessary to interview Kirkpatrick in private. Surely, this concerns me as the District Attorney, just as much as it does you. Surely you can trust me—"

Lingwell was growing angry and suspicious, and Wentworth hastened to cover up. "All right, Lingwell. You can stay. But I don't think we need the deputy warden. You can send for him again when we are through interviewing the prisoner."

District Attorney Lingwell agreed reluctantly, and sent the deputy warden away, after signing a receipt for the prisoner. As soon as the warden was gone, Lingwell turned brusquely to Wentworth and said: "Now, Woods, let's get this over—"

He stopped short, mouth agape, his wide eyes fixed on the ugly-snouted barrel of the snub nosed automatic that had appeared in the bogus G-man's hand. "W-what's the meaning—?"

"Sit down, Lingwell!" Wentworth barked. With his left hand he took the second automatic out of his shoulder clip, handed it to the ex-commissioner. "Keep him covered, Kirk."

It was characteristic of these two that neither had to say a word to the other. They both understood what was to be done. Speed of action would count now, and not words. While Kirkpatrick kept Lingwell covered, Wentworth rummaged in the desk till he found what he wanted. It was the embossed stationery of the District Attorney's office. He took a sheet of this paper, then found in another drawer the seal of the County of New York. Lingwell watched him, perspiring. "T-then you aren't a G-Man?"

Wentworth shook his head. He bent over the desk, writing swiftly with the pen from the desk set. Lingwell's eyes opened wide as he read the words taking shape on the paper:

> The prisoner, Stanley Kirkpatrick, is hereby transferred to the custody of the bearer, to be taken to Washington for questioning....

"Here!" he shouted. "You can't do that! Help!—"

HIS SHOUT was cut short by the hand of Commissioner Kirkpatrick, who had jumped around the desk and seized him. Kirkpatrick grinned at Wentworth. "What'll we do with him, Dick?"

"We'll have to tie him up till we get out of the building. I saw a pair of handcuffs in his desk drawer. Use those, and a couple of handkerchiefs for a gag. Sorry, Lingwell, but we've got to do this. Law of self-preservation, you know. We'll put you in the closet over there, and phone in when we've got away, to let the office know where you are."

Kirkpatrick had already snapped on the handcuffs, and was preparing the gag. Lingwell slumped in the chair, all the starch gone out of him. "My God, who are you? The city's in the grip of Tang-akhmut, and I thought you were from Washington and would help—"

"I'll help, all right," Wentworth tied him softly. "Depend on me. The true Mr. Woods should arrive in an hour or two. I'm afraid the Department of Justice won't be able to intervene, without the request of the governor. But I'll be working on the case."

He got the transfer finished, and riffled through a number of papers on the desk until he found Lingwell's signature. This he copied expertly, appending it to the bottom of the sheet he had written. "All right. Kirk," he said. "You go out first, and wait for me in the corridor. I'll be right with you. Leave the gag on the desk. I'll put it on when I'm through."

Kirkpatrick looked puzzled, but obeyed. As soon as the door had closed upon him, Wentworth said to Lingwell: "You'd better come into that closet without resistance. I'd hate to have to knock you on the head."

The district attorney nodded numbly, and rose. Wentworth led him to the closet, made him as comfortable as possible on the floor and prepared to put on the gag.

"B-but who are you?" Lingwell sputtered desperately. "You say you'll help the city. But who are you?"

Wentworth forced the gag between Lingwell's teeth, fastened it behind his back. Not till he was finished did he speak. "I promised that I'd help," he said softly. "And I will. I'm going to take up the battle against Tang-akhmut—if it's really he who's running this racket. And now, to convince you that I mean what I say, I'm going to tell you who I am."

He turned his back on Lingwell for a moment, and took from his pocket a chromium cigarette lighter. He flipped open the back of it, and pressed the flat, open end against the wall. When he removed the lighter from the wall, there remained upon the plaster, the bright red impression of a spider—the seal of the man who was feared by the underworld and hated by the police!

Lingwell had not been able to see what he was doing. Now Wentworth stepped aside, let the gagged district attorney see the imprint. Lingwell's eyes opened wide. Low, choked sounds came from his gagged mouth. He stared up at Wentworth in fascinated wonder.

"Yes," said Wentworth. "The Spider. The Spider gives you his word that he will join the fight against Tang-akhmut!"

And leaving Lingwell there he stepped out through the office to join Kirkpatrick. He had deliberately asked his friend to step out, because the ex-commissioner did not know that Richard Wentworth was the Spider. And Wentworth wasn't ready to have him know it yet.

They made their way out of the Criminal Courts Building without molestation. At the outer door of the district attorney's office, a guard stopped them, staring at Kirkpatrick. But the transfer that Wentworth had forged got them through without argument. Once in the street, they hailed a taxi, and the Spider barked: "Pennsylvania Station!"

Kirkpatrick looked at him questioningly. "We're going out of town, Dick?"

Wentworth smiled. "*You* are, old friend. You're going to my hunting lodge in the Catskills, to recuperate. You're in no condition for the war that's going to break out in this city tonight. Here's money—plenty of it. Thank God I was able to recover my fortune when I raided Tang-akhmut's headquarters last month. This will tide you over. And if Tang-akhmut is back, there may be a chance for us to clear ourselves."

Kirkpatrick laughed harshly. "Clear ourselves? Don't underestimate Tang-akhmut. If he's back, be sure he's got a carefully laid plan. He probably expects you to take the initiative against him, and has a clever trap laid for you."

"I'll have to chance that, Kirk," Wentworth told him softly.

CHAPTER 2
A PATH TO PHARAOH

THE EXCLUSIVE Fifth Avenue jewelry establish-
ment of Robillard & Co. was unusually quiet this afternoon. Though crowds of people were passing outside, few came
to make purchases here. For the wealthy of the city had learned
through connections downtown of the spread of typhoid, and
had fled the city. The news had been kept from the masses of
people for fear of creating a panic. And those masses could not
afford to purchase the expensive trinkets sold by the Robillard
firm.

Diagonally across the street, however, the immense department store of Fremont and Tynan was doing a rushing business.
Shoppers were hurrying in and out, unaware as yet that danger
hung over the city like a black cloak of doom.

Pierre Robillard sat in the musty office at the rear of the store,
his fine old eyes dulled by some inner fear. His long, closely
shaven face was pale. His gaze strayed out through the store to
the long, sleek limousine that pulled up in front of the door. He
watched the swarthy, oriental chauffeur come around and open
the door, saw the tall, darkly beautiful woman who descended
and crossed the curb to the entrance. He did not arise to meet
her, and he betrayed no enthusiasm at the prospect of making
a sale. In fact, he knew that this woman had not come to buy
anything.

He watched tensely as she made her way through the aisles of
showcases with their glittering displays of jewelry. The woman

waved away the clerks who hastened to serve her, and made directly for the office.

At last, Pierre Robillard arose. His old face was stern, set in hard lines. His voice was husky with emotion. "I told you that I would not agree to your terms. Why do you return?" he demanded.

The woman smiled coldly. "I return," she said, "because you were given until today to accept the terms of the Snakemen. Whether your answer is yes or no, I have come for it!" From her purse she took a brass plaque upon which was stamped the figure of a coiled cobra. "Here is the plaque, if you have decided to change your mind. The price has been raised to fifty thousand dollars!"

Pierre Robillard's hands clenched with emotion. "You witch!" he cried. "I will never pay. Get out, or I will call the police!"

The fixed smile on her lips did not alter. "Before you call the police," she suggested, "it would be better that you call your home."

"What do you mean?" he asked dully.

BEFORE SHE could reply, the telephone on his desk tinkled, and he picked it up automatically. As he listened to the message coming over the wire, all the blood drained from his face, and the hand that held the receiver trembled. At last he said brokenly into the transmitter. "I will see what I can do."

He put down the phone, looked up haggardly into the woman's eyes. "What have you done with my granddaughter—with little Elaine?" he asked huskily.

The woman nodded. "I suppose that was your home, inform-

21

RICHARD WENTWORTH

ing you of the child's disappearance. Nothing has been done to her—as yet. I merely await your answer." She tapped the plaque significantly.

"You've kidnapped Elaine!" Robillard breathed. "Just as you

kidnapped Lawrence Fremont from across the street, and a dozen others!"

She shrugged. "Many people have found that it is easier—and safer—to meet the terms of the Snake-master at once. What is your answer?"

Pierre Robillard burst out desperately: "Give me time. I'll raise the money. I haven't any such sum in cash. It's all tied up in my stock—"

"I'm sorry," she told him coldly. "We must have it at once."

"I'll give you jewelry. Take what you please from my stock. Only give me back Elaine. Her father and mother are dead. I've cared for her for three years now, since she was seven. I—couldn't bear it if anything happened to her. I—can't bear to think of her in strange hands. For God's sake, give me time to raise the money, or take jewelry—"

The woman's long eyes were veiled under dark lashes. "You should have considered all that yesterday, when I stated the Snake-master's terms. We want no jewelry. I can give you two hours to produce the cash—no more!"

The old man's face twisted in a sudden surge of anger, and

his cheeks flushed hotly. "Damn you!" he almost shrieked, and took a quick step toward her, his hands outstretched to throttle. "My Elaine—"

He had not noticed the tall man who had left the limousine and followed the woman through the store. This man now appeared in the doorway just behind her, and he pushed past the woman. His face was sinister, dangerous, topped by an incongruous shock of pure white hair. A livid scar disfigured his cheek and forehead, running down across his left eye, which was no eye at all, but only an empty socket. His one good eye burned with a deadly malevolence. Thin lips twisted into a ghastly smile as he said to the woman: "This man is troublesome, Princess Issoris?"

Pierre Robillard paused in midstride, staring at the blued-steel revolver which the one-eyed man held. He whirled, leaped toward his desk, where a gun lay in the drawer. But he had hardly taken a single step before the revolver in the one-eyed man's hand barked. A jet of flame, the whine of a slug, and Pierre Robillard screamed, pitched forward across his desk with a shattered spine.

His body slipped off the desk to the floor, and he lay on his face, twitching. The Princess Issoris looked down at the dying man without a tremor. The old man's voice sounded faint and far away, thickened by the bubble of blood at his lips: "Elaine! Poor El—"

There was a rattle in his throat, he stiffened convulsively, and then relaxed. He was dead.

The Princess Issoris turned on her heel without a single backward glance, and strode out of the office, with the one-eyed man behind her. The clerks shrank from the brandished revolver, gave way before them. The two passed unmolested to the curb, and entered the limousine, which pulled away at once.

Outside the store, people passed undisturbed. The single shot in this city of noises and strange disturbances had not attracted any attention. It was several minutes before the clerks mustered up enough courage to come to the door. By then the limousine was out of sight....

AT ABOUT the same time that this cold-blooded murder was taking place, Richard Wentworth was striding somberly across Thirty-Fourth Street, in the shadow of the tall Empire State building. He had put Kirkpatrick on a train for the Catskills, seen him safely off, then had gone into the wash room of the station and had there removed the white tufts from his eyebrows and the patches of white from his temples. He took the plates from his nostrils, allowed his shoulders to straighten a bit; and when he looked into the mirror, Mr. Woods of Washington had disappeared. His own clean-cut, purposeful face stared back at him.

Wentworth pulled his hat brim down lower over his face, and left the station. Now he was Richard Wentworth once more, fair prey for the police. But he disdained any further disguise. In the teeming city, distracted as it was by the strange crimes occurring with breath-taking rapidity, people would have no time to look for Richard Wentworth, fugitive from justice. His very boldness in walking the streets would be his best safeguard. And the things that he had to do today required that he appear in his own identity.

He turned into the Empire State Building, went up in the high-speed elevator to the forty-seventh floor, where he entered an office marked:

FENTON & BANNISTER
Private Investigators

A month ago he had hired this firm to conduct discreet inquiries as to the possible whereabouts of Tang-akhmut. The Living Pharaoh's complex criminal organization had been badly broken up by the Spider at that time, and it was to be expected that Tang-akhmut had either left for another country or gone into hiding somewhere in the United States. One thing was certain—that the bitter, vengeful Man from the East would not rest until he had recruited other forces of evil, and until he had returned to attempt once more to carry out the ambitious, merciless plans which had been interrupted by the Spider.

Thus far, Freddy Fenton and Jack Bannister had succeeded in unearthing very little in the way of dues as to the doings or whereabouts of Tang-akhmut. They were deeply in the debt of Richard Wentworth, and would gladly have worked for him without compensation. But he paid them well, notwithstanding, in the hope that by continuing their assiduous search they would stumble upon a trail that he himself could take up.

Now, as he entered the office, Freddy Fenton himself sprang up from the desk in one of the two inner offices, and came out past his secretary's desk in the reception room. The door of the inner office had been open, and Fenton had seen him come in. Fenton was a stocky man in his early thirties, a former patrolman on the New York police force, who had been financed in this business by Wentworth. His face expressed worried concern.

"Don't tell me that you've been walking the streets like that!" he exclaimed. "It's true that there are no pictures of you available, but there are plenty of people in New York who know you by sight, and in case it's news to you, there's a murder warrant out for a certain person by the name of Richard Wentworth!"

The Spider smiled tolerantly. "I'll get by, Freddie. I came in to put you and Bannister to work on a new line—"

They were walking into the inner office, past the secretary, who continued her typing in tactful silence, without looking up. Fenton interrupted. "I'll tell you, Mr. Wentworth, you just came in at the right time. Jack Bannister phoned in not ten minutes ago, that he's on his way up with some news of—you-know-who!"

"Tang-akhmut?" Wentworth asked sharply.

"Right. It seems he was down in some dive on the East Side, and he picked up a couple of rumors. The underworld is all upset about these mysterious happenings in the city. There are lots of stories going around. Bannister didn't say what he got, but he'll be here—"

FENTON WAS interrupted by the sudden opening of the outer door, and the abrupt appearance of Bannister. Fenton's partner was tall, with wavy blond hair, and an air of youthful eagerness. He was manifestly very excited, and when he saw Wentworth he hurried over, exclaiming: "Chief! I think I've got something! It's big! So big that I'm afraid of it myself!

"There are stories going the rounds that Tang-akhmut is back—with a crew of the worst murderers and cutthroats this side of Suez. There's supposed to be a one-eyed guy that led a massacre of white men in Indo-China, and a snake-doctor that was sent to French Guiana for poisoning a whole village, and—"

The secretary's rapid typing had been drumming a low, rapid accompaniment to Bannister's quick flow of excited speech. Now, abruptly, it ceased, and the girl's voice was raised in a horrified screech. Bannister, who was standing facing Wentworth and Fenton, with his back to the outer door, broke off and started to turn. Wentworth caught a glimpse of a swarthy, oily countenance in the doorway, of a crouching man, of an upflung arm. Light slithered on a shining blade of steel that swirled as the upflung arm hurled it.

Bannister uttered a choked cry of pain, and staggered. The knife was embedded in his back, thrown with deadly aim. It had pierced his heart. The young private investigator gasped, and his jaw fell slack. He buckled at the knees, and started to crumple to the floor. He was dead on his feet!

Wentworth's hand streaked up and down from his shoulder holster, and an automatic appeared, spitting lead even while Bannister was falling. The evil face of the knife thrower had moved swiftly from the doorway as its owner swung into flight after accomplishing his mission. But Wentworth's gun was quicker. The first slug from the heavy gun shattered the murderer's head like an eggshell, spattering brains and blood on the floor and on the open door. The knife thrower's body was hurled backward into the corridor.

Wentworth leaped to the door, gun held forward, seeking any accomplices. There were none. The man was evidently alone, or any companions had fled. Bleak-eyed, the Spider eyed the assassin, a Hindu, then turned back into the office. The secretary had dumped over her typewriter in a faint, and Freddy Fenton was kneeling over the pitiful body of his partner. He raised dull eyes to the Spider. "God, Mr. Wentworth, he's—dead! He was only a kid. He had—so much to live for!"

Wentworth said harshly: "He learned too much. He must have been followed here." He bent swiftly and felt the dead lad's pulse, nodded. "He's dead. I'll see that his family is taken care of." Wentworth's voice thickened. "That's all I can do for him now—except to get the one behind that knife thrower!"

Fenton exclaimed suddenly: "Mr. Wentworth! You can't stay here! The police'll be up in a second. They're bound to recognize you. Better get out. Leave your gun. I'll say I shot that murderer."

Wentworth agreed. He wiped the fingerprints from his automatic, gave it to Fenton. "Take care of yourself, Freddy," he said softly. "Drop all cases, and keep to the office. I don't want you getting killed too."

Fenton's jaw jutted. "He was my partner, Mr. Wentworth—"

"That's all right, Freddy. But I'm going to handle this myself from here on. Keep clear of it, and leave me a free hand!"

There was the sound of excited voices out in the corridor, shouts for police. Wentworth pressed Fenton's hand, and went through into the inner office, opened a door that led him into a side corridor. Several office doors along the hall were open, and men stared out looking for the source of the shot. Wentworth moved back down the hall toward the elevators, joined a group of people who were standing at a good distance, looking at the body of the Hindu outside Fenton & Bannister's office. None went too near. While they watched, an elevator reached the floor, and a patrolman emerged, asking loudly: "What's happened here?—"

He broke off, ran to the dead Hindu. Wentworth seized the

The Asiatic, catapulted
backward, crashed into the
one-eyed announcer.

opportunity, stepped into the cage. The operator was goggling past the crowd, and the cop lifted his head, shouted: "No one leaves this floor till the sergeant comes. This is murder!"

WENTWORTH WAS already in the cage, behind the operator. He gave him a shove, sent him stumbling out into the corridor, and shut the door. He pulled over the lever, and the cage shot downward with whizzing, breathless speed. Wentworth sent it all the way down, past the main floor lobby, and got out in the basement concourse. He left the cage, walked leisurely out, strolled past the radio car that had just pulled in at the curb, and flagged a taxi.

"Central Park West," he ordered coolly.

The driver tooled the cab into a left turn up Fifth Avenue. "What's going on back there?" he asked over his shoulder. "Wherever you go today you see police cars and ambulances. They don't let you near enough to get a look, and there ain't a word about it in the papers or on the radio. Gawd, what's all this that's goin' on in the city, mister?"

Wentworth shrugged. "If I knew, I'd feel a lot better too," he said.

He left the cab before an apartment house on Central Park West, and ascended to the third floor. This was the apartment of his fiancée, Nita van Sloan. All morning he had been worried about her. If Tang-akhmut was back, he would surely first attempt to ferret out Nita's address, for the so-called Living Pharaoh well knew that he could best strike at Wentworth through the woman he loved.

Nita had gone along the road of peril with Richard Wentworth bravely, hoping ever that the time would come when he would forsake his chosen career, and would be free to live in the comfort of a home, like other men. But she gloried perhaps as much as he did in the perpetual danger that beset their lives; and sometimes she felt that she would not love Wentworth as much, if he did not love danger more.

Wentworth smiled happily when she met him at the door. He saw at a glance that nothing had happened here—as yet. In the living room, his tall Sikh servant, Ram Singh, was at the telephone. Ram Singh held the instrument out to him. *"Wah,* master," he said in his rich baritone voice. "You have come at the right moment. Here is one who would speak with thee!"

Wentworth frowned, took the phone. "Strange," he said, covering the mouthpiece with his hand, "that anyone should know I can be reached here."

Nita's brow was suddenly troubled. "Oh, Dick, don't answer. I have a peculiar feeling. I'm afraid—"

He laughed, threw an arm around her shoulder, and spoke into the phone. "Who is this?"

A high-pitched voice answered. "Richard Wentworth! You seek the Man from the East, while he wreaks havoc in your city. I am one who would be your friend. Go at once to the department store of Fremont and Tynan, There you will see those who serve Tang-akhmut!"

Wentworth tautened. "Who is this?" he demanded.

"One who hates the Living Pharaoh even as you do. Hurry. There is little time. Even now you may be late!"

There was a click, and the line went dead.

NITA HAD been standing close to Wentworth, and she heard every word. Her face was pale. "Dick! Don't go. I had a premonition—"

Her voice died as she met his eyes. She knew him well. She knew that he would go, that nothing she could say would stop him.

Ram Singh said eagerly: "Let us go quickly, master. I would meet once more that swine who calls himself the Living Pharaoh—"

Wentworth shook his head. "And leave Nita alone? No. You will remain here. Get me another automatic!"

Nita put a hand on his sleeve. "Dick! This may be a trap. How did that person know that you were here? Maybe they want to get you out in the open—"

He laughed. "Well, they'll have their way. If it's a trap, I'll walk into it with my eyes open. It's the only way, darling!"

Swiftly he related to her the events of the day. "Everything points to the fact that Tang-akhmut is back with a more dangerous crew than ever before. Those isolated killings, the typhoid infections spreading through the city—those are merely the introductory blows. Something big, something terrible, is scheduled to happen soon. Maybe it'll be at Fremont and Tynan's. And I want to be there.

"If you have to go out for any reason, Nita, use the secret entrance through the next apartment. And if we should get out of touch with each other, come to the prearranged meeting place at Yang Chung's in Chinatown. We can trust him. It was through him that I was able to rescue Kirk. Now, good-by,

34

Nita darling. Let's hope that this will be the end of the war with Tang-akhmut."

"*Wah!*" said Ram Singh lugubriously. "Let us hope that the war does not leave Tang-akhmut supreme!" He handed Wentworth the automatic, followed him as far as the door. Then he returned to the living room to stand beside Nita, who was watching out of the window.

"Perhaps," he said hopefully, "there will be an attempt against you, *memsahib*. I would like a good fight…."

CHAPTER 3
MARCH OF THE LEPERS

THE MAN was running blindly, stumbling, palpitating with fright. In the gloomy dusk of the bleak autumn afternoon his face appeared weird, distorted; and his mouth hung open, drawing in great gulps of air. Wild, terror-stricken eyes burned from sockets that were sunk deep in folds of mottled, unwholesome flesh.

The Saturday afternoon throngs on upper Fifth Avenue pushed out of his way, forming a lane through which the terrified man staggered. Women paled at sight of his repulsive countenance, and uttered little shrieks of revulsion. Men fended him off with elbows.

A uniformed patrolman at the corner toward which the man was running heard the commotion and started down the street, frowning. The cop's nerves were on edge, for only a little while ago there had been a murder across the street. Pierre Robillard had been shot in cold blood. Now this—

Abruptly, the terrified man stopped short twenty feet from the corner, in front of the entrance to the great Fifth Avenue Department Store of Fremont and Tynan. Here he seemed to totter for a moment, then he raised his head and screamed in a high-pitched, raucous voice: "The lepers! The lepers are coming! *God, the lepers!*"

He swayed, seemed about to fall, but remained on his feet, stumbling toward the chastely modernistic entrance of Fremont & Tynan's. The crowd of Fifth Avenue strollers and shoppers had given way before him, forming a cleared space around him. And now it became evident that the man was wounded in some way, for there was blood on the pavement where he had run, and blood was dripping down from somewhere under the swallow-tailed coat that be clutched tightly about his stout figure. The blood splashed in great globules to the sidewalk at his feet.

The uniformed flunky in front of the department store stepped forward to stop the man from entering. At the same time the uniformed patrolman from the corner pushed through the throng to the cleared circle. Both the flunkey and the cop seized the man at the same time. It was the doorman who first got a clear look at the man's face, and it was the flunkey who first released his grip on the unfortunate's sleeve, recoiling in horror from the close glimpse of the man's face.

The cop swung the man around, shouted: "Here, you, what's happened—*my God!*"

The policeman's hand fell away from the other's sleeve with

as much speed as had the doorman's a second before. For the face that peered out from under the matted gray hair was scabrous, mottled, with ugly white patches and red feverish streaks.

From the man's lips came once again the high-pitched, jumbled sounds which shaped themselves into almost indistinguishable words: *"The lepers! The lepers are coming!"*

The cop stepped backward involuntarily from the shrieking man, and his eyes dropped to the ground, where a pool of blood was rapidly forming, then up to the spot where the man's hand was pressing against his side.

The doorman sidled around toward the cop, whispered in awed voice: "God, it's Mr. Fremont, himself! *And he's got leprosy!*"

THE POLICEMAN gasped. He had patrolled this corner for quite a while now, and many times in the past he had seen Lawrence Fremont arrive in his six-teen-cylinder limousine, to spend an hour or so in the executive office of the huge department store that he headed. But he had not recognized in this scabrous, repulsive individual the ordinarily immaculate Lawrence Fremont.

It was true, he recalled, that Fremont had been missing for a week, and there had been a country-wide search for him.

It had been thought that he was either the victim of a kidnapping plot, or that he had been afflicted with amnesia. And now here he was!

The patrolman's face paled, and his eyes riveted fascinatedly to the figure of Lawrence Fremont. The crowd about them had heard what the doorman said, and a swift, agitated whisper went around: "It's Fremont himself! God, what's happened to him? Look, he's wounded! Is that really leprosy?"

No one dared to extend a helping hand to the tottering man. Fremont's voice had weakened, and he was barely whispering his wild, feverish refrain: "The lepers—the lepers are coming!" And with that he crumpled, and slid in a quivering heap to the sidewalk, his clawing fingers making a weird pattern in the coating of blood upon the pavement.

Still they all kept their distance. The dreadful mention of the word *leprosy* had placed an icy chill on the hearts of all those people who had just been strolling up the Avenue so gaily. A hush descended upon them as they stared at the pitiful crumpled heap on the ground—the figure of the man who was known to many of them as the greatest retail merchant prince in the east.

Fremont was trying to push himself up on one elbow, and his horribly distorted face was turned upward now, no longer shrieking, but his lips were moving desperately, spasmodically, as if he were trying to impart some message.

The street had become filled by this time, and a police prowl car pulled up at the curb, its crew leaping out to investigate. A plainclothes precinct man pushed through the crowd too and the patrolman who had been first on the scene explained in hushed tones: "It's Lawrence Fremont. He's wounded, and he's—"

The plainclothes detective barked: "Hell, he's dying. Why

don't you help him!" and bent down to give the dying man a hand. It was not till then that he noticed the white, mottled patches on Fremont's face, the scaly sores that proclaimed the presence of leprosy. The detective jerked his hand back as if he had touched a hot stove. "Lord! He's—"

"That's what I was trying to tell you, Struve," the patrolman said. "He's got—leprosy!"

Struve wavered. Duty called for him to help the wounded man, to try to discover what it was he was whispering through suddenly bloody lips. But the fear of the dread disease held him back.

Fremont reached up a bony, emaciated hand, and tried to clutch at Struve's trousers leg. The detective kicked at the hand, shouting: "Don't touch me!"

Some one in the crowd yelled: "God, get an ambulance. Call the hospital!"

Fremont's struggle to get up and to speak had weakened him, and he fell back to the pavement. His coat slipped open, and a great gasp went up from the throng. There was a knife hilt sticking out from his body, just below the fifth rib, and it was from this wound that the river of blood was flowing.

But that great gasp of dismay and horror that came like a gust of cold wind from the suddenly awe-struck crowd was caused by something different. Exactly in the center of Fremont's white-skinned chest there had been carved a bloody circle, about six inches in diameter. It must have been cut with some kind of wedge-shaped instrument, for the skin had not grown together, thus causing the line of the circle to stand out in ghastly, raw contrast to his otherwise pallid skin.

And perpendicularly through the axis of that circle had been cut the twining, sinuous figure of a cobra! The thing was so life-like that it seemed to stare out at the crowd with its small wicked eyes, as if it were lying there in Fremont's very body!

MEN BACKED away from the triply gruesome sight, and women uttered cries of terror. One woman screamed, and fainted. Now, shoppers coming out of the department store, found their way blocked by the hideous man who lay in their path, and pushed back into the store.

And Fremont lay there, gasping out his life, repulsive and horrid on the threshold of death, his blood-flecked lips forming words that no one heard. Strove, the detective, was peering down fearfully at Fremont's writing figure, as the patrolman

told him: "It's the queerest ever, Struve. I seen him running, and then the crowd blocked him from my view. When I come up here, he was shouting something about the lepers coming, and that was all I could catch—"

Just then they were literally hurled aside by a tall, well-knit man who had battled his way through the crowd into the cleared circle. Neither the patrolman nor the detective recognized in the poised, assured figure the man whom the police department was hunting everywhere—Richard Wentworth. They were too much under the strain of the terrible thing they were seeing.

Wentworth exclaimed: "Don't you see he's trying to tell you something!" Bleakly he dropped to one knee beside the dying Fremont. So that telephone call hadn't been a hoax. It might still be a trap. And he had come just a bit too late, as the unknown voice on the phone had said he might—or hadn't he come too late? Was there something more to follow?

Gently he raised Fremont to a sitting position, regardless of the blood that sported on his immaculate business suit.

Struve bent excitedly, grasped his hand. "Look at there, you fool. Good God, don't you see that man's a leper!"

Wentworth impatiently shook off Struve's hand. His eyes, suddenly narrowed, were fixed on the hideous symbol of the coiled cobra in the bloody circle, cut into Fremont's chest. His long, sensitive fingers reached out to touch the festering scab that was forming over the cruel mark.

Fremont groaned, and a rattle sounded in his throat. His bloodshot gaze lifted to Wentworth's, and he gasped: "The lepers—"

41

The words ended in a fit of coughing, and Wentworth raised him a little higher, probed down toward the knife handle in the man's side. He dared not withdraw that knife, for that would mean a swift hemorrhage resulting in instant death. Instead, he whipped a handkerchief out of his pocket, pressed it around the keen blade, stanching the flow of blood.

Fremont's coughing fit ceased, and he gasped for breath, seemed to be gathering his last remaining energy to speak again. Wentworth glanced down at his haggard, sore-infested face, and asked softly; "Who did this to you, Fremont?"

An ambulance bell was clanging in the distance, a radio car siren was screaming, and a babble of voices rose all about them. But Fremont did not appear to be conscious of anything but the words he was trying to force out of his lips:

"My store—is—doomed! Leper men—are going—to raid it. For God's sake—clear—the store—I should have bought—the Shield of the Cobra—*Ah, God, I'm dy*—"

His voice ended in a dreadful whistling shriek, and he fell back in Wentworth's arms—dead.

THE AMBULANCE swung wildly in to the curb, and a young intern leaped out, just as the police radio car from the other corner squealed to a halt facing it.

Wentworth paid no attention to all that. His mind was grappling with a problem. Leprosy! First it had been typhoid, now leprosy. Fremont had been missing only a week. How, in God's name, could he have reached this advanced stage of the dreadful disease in so short a time? There was that cable from the Paris Sûreté. It had mentioned something about a leper colony.

But leprosy certainly didn't flourish this fast.

Wentworth felt numb. Tang-akhmut was striking power-fully, ruthlessly. Blow after blow was

being delivered at a dazed city. And the Spider knew Tang-akhmut well enough to understand that this was but a prelude. Something spectacular would follow—something that would be calculated to drive the city into submission. From what quarter that attack would come, what shape it would take, he could not guess.

Himself, he had no fear of leprosy. He knew that it was unlikely that one would contract the disease by merely touching a leper—unless he had an open cut or sore. But all these people who were watching in stunned wonder did not know that. Already the whisper was running through the huge crowd. Already the grim specter of panic was stalking among them. It needed only some bold blow on the part of the Living Pharaoh to throw the whole city in chaos.

Wentworth gently laid the dead man back on the pavement, and rose to his feet. The young intern pushed into the cleared circle, and stopped stock still, looking down at the disfigured face of Fremont. Then he looked up at Wentworth, who nodded grimly. "Yes, doctor. It's—what you think it is!"

The intern's lips formed the involuntary question: "Leprosy?"

"That's right."

"But that's impossible. We haven't had a case—"

Wentworth waved him aside, swung to Struve. "Look here, you've got to clear the store of people. Something's going to happen. Fremont said—"

He was interrupted by sudden shouts of horror from the crowd. People began to shoulder past, running in panic-stricken fright from something he could not yet see. Men and women rushed by them, pressed by those behind, apparently fleeing from something that was approaching from the same direction from which Fremont had come.

Struve shouted: "What the hell's the matter? Where you running—"

But Wentworth, who was taller, and could see over the heads of the throng, had already glimpsed the thing that had caused the panic. There fifty feet down the street, came a group of silent men. They marched four abreast, in perfect step, with enough space between them so that they stretched from the curb to the building line.

These men held no weapons. But they were bare to the waist in spite of the chill autumn weather, and on the chest of each of them was graven a device exactly similar to the one on the chest of the dead Lawrence Fremont. Against their white, hideously scaly skins, the ugly design with the live-looking coiled cobra stood out in ghastly relief. Their faces were covered by tight-fitting rubber hoods, in which slits had been cut for the mouth, nose and eyes; so that they appeared to be some ungainly monsters sprung alive out of a loathsome nightmare.

The Spider's blood chilled. This then, was the culminating blow in the planned campaign of Tang-akhmut—a raid of lepers!

NO WORD came from those silent marching, half-naked men. The sidewalk was clear now, and Wentworth faced the first ranks of the raiders across the dead body of Lawrence Fremont. Behind him, Struve and the other policemen shakily drew their guns, while the young intern hastily backed away toward the ambulance.

Struve shouted hoarsely: "Halt, in the name of the law! Who are you?"

He might as well have addressed the wind. He got no answer. Those hooded men, with the emblem of the cobra branded on their chests, marched inexorably forward, keeping step to some inaudible beat, their arms bent at the elbows, and held rigid, so that the hands were extended in front of them.

Struve repeated his hoarse command to halt, but they did not seem to have heard. Now they were twenty feet away, and Wentworth could see burning eyes peering out at him from behind the slits in the black rubber masks.

Struve had his revolver out now, and he stepped in front of Wentworth, shouting: "Stop, damn you! Stop or I'll shoot!"

Still the lepers came on. And Struve, uttering a hysterical yell, leaped forward, his revolver roaring six times in quick succession, the shots echoing down the street. After him, the three uniformed policemen came running, firing also as they ran.

The fusillade of shots from the police mowed down the first and second ranks of the lepers. Each of those in the foremost ranks fell with three or four bullets in his body. But those behind coolly stepped over their fallen companions, and marched inexorably forward. These men had no fear of death!

Struve and the policemen stopped short, their guns empty. Never in their experience had they encountered a situation like this. In the hysteria of the moment they had fired at unarmed men, had shot down more than half a dozen. And now, the others came at them, inscrutable behind rubber masks, with hideously diseased flesh, and with gruesome symbols on their bodies.

It was too much for the policemen. They gave way to panic, and turned to run. Struve turned to follow them, his face contorted into a gargoyle of fear. And it was then that the leper men swung into action. Hideous yells broke from their throats, and those in the lead leaped at the luckless detective, their fingers curved like talons to gouge and scratch at his flesh.

Struve stumbled, and the monsters were upon him, raking his face with long, black fingernails. Strove screamed, and kicked, lashing out in a frenzy of panic. But as suddenly as they had leaped upon him, the leper men left him. His face was furrowed by a dozen raking scratches, and it seemed that that was all they had wanted to accomplish. For now, their yells dying down, they marched forward again, stepping over Struve as if he did not exist.

WENTWORTH HAD not joined the police in the attack on the leper men. His mind, working with the lightning swiftness of pure instinct, had grasped in a flash of revelation, what was the purpose of these silently marching, leprous figures.

While Struve raced to meet them in blind, unthinking action, Wentworth swung toward the doorman of the department store, behind whom cowered dozens of patrons who had stopped there on the way out, transfixed by sudden terror.

"Quick!" Wentworth shouted, above the crackling reports of the police revolvers. "Get out of the store. Get away as fast as you can. Those men intend to spread leprosy. Run!"

They shrank away from him, for they had seen with their own eyes how he had touched the leprous body of the dead Fremont. These were mostly women shoppers, and they began a cacophony of screams and shrill hysterical laughter. Wentworth glowered at them, seized the doorman by the shoulder and spun him through the doorway.

"Get going" he snapped. "You fools! Do you want to be infected with leprosy? Get away while you can! I'll hold these monsters back as long as possible, till the store is emptied!"

Under the lash of his words they began to retreat, then broke into a full run toward the other exits.

Wentworth swung about, and his lips tightened as he saw the prone body of Strove, with his face hideously scratched, and the leper men marching over him in their silent advance. The uniformed policemen who had fled were down the street, desperately racing to reload their revolvers, fumbling the cartridges in their wild haste. Further behind them, the massed crowds were watching in fascinated horror. They had seen those long nails of the leper men rake the face of the detective, and they saw how the monsters were now advancing toward the store.

The huge doors of Fremont and Tynan's store could not be

47

closed quickly. At the closing hour they generally took fully five minutes to roll into place and to lock. There was nothing to stop the lepers from invading the store—except the lone man who stood there, tall and immovable, facing the silent advance.

Wentworth's arms crossed over his chest in a motion so swift that the red, lustful eyes behind the rubber hoods could hardly follow them. And an automatic appeared in each steady fist, barking in cool, unhurried tempo, spitting slugs at the advancing leper cohort.

Whereas Strove and the policemen had shot with the frantic speed of sudden panic, Wentworth fired with calculating accuracy. The drumming of the two guns sounded almost like the staccato tattoo of a machine gun; and each shot counted. A leper fell each time the triggers clicked.

The deep-throated reverberations of his gunfire rolled down the Avenue with the dull thunder of doom. The ranks of the leper men were decimated. Nine shots in each automatic took swift toll of the attacking monsters. Wentworth stood straddle-legged over the dead body of Lawrence Fremont, and emptied his guns with deliberate care.

The first and second ranks of hooded men dropped under the withering barrage, and the third and the fourth. The sidewalk was littered with their bodies. Yet they came on, never swerving, never stopping, like dreadful automatons that knew not the meaning of death. It was a sight such as had seldom—if ever—been witnessed in a civilized land. One might have thought that those advancing ranks were not ranks of mortals, but some weird devils come to earth—except for the fact that bullets could kill them.

Even Wentworth experienced a queer chill of amazement as he saw that his barrage had failed to stop the advance. Those in the rear ranks merely stepped over the bodies of their dead fellows, and marched straight toward him.

Now they were within a few feet, and they broke into a shambling run that sent them in an engulfing wave around Wentworth. Long, black fingernails reached to claw at him, and smelly, naked bodies surrounded him. He guessed that those fingernails carried the bacillus of leprosy, and once they had raked him, the dreadful germ would become part of his blood stream.

HE FOUGHT with the cool deliberation of the trained fighting machine that he was—fought to keep those clawing fingers from reaching his face. His fists, gripping the clubbed automatics, lashed out with the perfect timing of pistons, striking heads, wrists, elbows, keeping a small clear circle about him. His eyes flashed with the excitement of battle which was like the breath of life to Richard Wentworth.

Had he himself been alone involved in this, he might have enjoyed the fray even more; but there gnawed at the back of his mind the thought of the hundreds of women in the great department store who would be exposed to those infected claws if he allowed the leper men to pass too soon. So he fought on, knowing that he could not for long avoid the scraping fingernail of the monsters who swarmed around him, but fighting for time—time for those within the store to escape.

Bony hands clutched at his coat, at his trouser legs, raked the air in quest of the skin of his face. His clubbed guns smashed into the attackers, and a small pile of writhing bodies grew at his feet. These men were not armed with weapons, and it seemed almost unsportsmanlike to have fired at them, and now to slug them with clubbed revolvers. But the realization of the dreadful bacilli they carried under their fingernails drove all such qualms from his mind.

Now, a hand gripped at his trouser cuff, tried to raise it to expose his leg, to rake it. Wentworth kicked out hard, and felt his shoe smash against bone. The clutching grip fell away, but Wentworth was caught off balance, and a shove from another hand sent him tumbling backward.

Grunts of triumph went up from the massed attackers, and clawed hands reached down for his face. Wentworth desperately twisted away, lashed out with both feet, won himself a moment's respite. By now the policemen had completed loading their revolvers, and a hail of slugs tore into the hooded men. They fell away from Wentworth, dropping all around him.

Only a few of the lepers were left alive, and these few obstinately attempted to reach the store entrance.

It was incredible—almost as if they were a suicide club of some sort, pledged to die. They had no weapons, yet they marched against blazing guns.

Wentworth's eyes were puzzled as he jackknifed to his feet, lunged after the half dozen who had won through into the store. Behind him, the policemen, whose guns were once more emptied, came on the run, wearing dazed, frightened expressions. Out in the street, a police riot car had screamed to a halt, and police with machine guns and tear gas bombs leaped down, raced toward the store after Wentworth.

But Wentworth was already inside, feverishly slapping fresh clips into his automatics. He got them loaded, and stopped, staring in shocked silence at the scene that spread itself before him in the aisles of the main floor.

CHAPTER 4
THE PRINCESS OF EVIL

THE FREMONT and Tynan Department Store took up the entire block from Fifth to Sixth Avenue. As one entered through the superbly modernistic Fifth Avenue entrance, there was a short arcade, lined on either side by ultra-fashionable, glass-enclosed, individual departments where the latest importations in cosmetics and dainty silks were sold. Then the arcade opened in a sort of balcony which ran around all four sides of the building, some seven feet wide. This balcony contained the book and stationery departments, and then there was a descent of three or four steps to the main floor, in wide aisles with convenient benches at every few steps.

It was on the balcony that Wentworth had stopped short, gazing in consternation down into the main floor.

The huge crowd of women shoppers had not left the building!

They were being herded toward the center of the floor by other groups of hooded leprous, half-naked men, who had come in from Sixth Avenue and by the side street entrances while the main group attacked on the Fifth Avenue side. The women, with a few men shoppers interspersed, were running about through the aisles in wild, blind panic. Shrieks, hysterical cries, moans of utter terror filled the building as the silent leper men crowded in against them, bony talons ripping and scraping at soft skins and leaving dreadful furrows where the leprosy-infected fingernails tore bloody scratches in their faces, on their breasts and arms.

It was like some ghastly scene that might have been transported from the nethermost depths of Dante's Inferno. The few men among the shoppers offered a feeble resistance to the grisly claws of the attackers. Many of the women lay fainting on the floor, trampled upon by the herd. Other women had snatched up umbrellas and walking sticks from the counters in that department, and were defending themselves as best they could. But the great majority of them crouched in panic at this sudden, unexplained attack, shielding their faces with arms and hands.

The leper men danced about them in unholy silence, striking aside their arms and ripping at their faces with long fingernails. The pandemonium of terror-laden sound that filled the building was ear-splitting.

Wentworth ripped out a low-voiced oath. There were at least a hundred of the leper men, and there was little that a single individual could do against them.

He raised his automatics, and shot carefully, swiftly, bringing down one of the hooded monsters with each slug.

It required superb marksmanship, for that crowd was in constant movement, and it would have been easy to hit one of the innocent women by mistake. But Wentworth exhausted his two clips with uncanny skill, finding a mark each time he pulled the trigger. His shooting had no effect on the leper men. The survivors continued their monstrous assault upon the crowd as if nothing had happened.

He lowered his empty guns with a feeling of defeat. Such defiance of death was absolutely incomprehensible. He had never witnessed it before, even when he had led troops in mad assault upon an impregnable enemy position during the Great War.

Bleak-eyed, he swung around at the sound of rushing feet, and saw the police riot squad loping on to the balcony from the arcade. They were led by ruddy-faced, white-haired Captain Kiernan, whom Wentworth knew by name. Kiernan stared in bewildered consternation at the devilish scene below.

WENTWORTH POINTED at the tear gas bombs carried by the members of the squad. "Tear gas!" he shouted. "Use it quickly!"

"But the women—they'll get it too!"

"Can't be helped. Hurry, man! Every second you delay means that more of those women are being doomed to leprosy!"

He seized a gas bomb from one of the men, and hurled it down on the floor. The missile shattered, and sharp, cutting fumes spread. Kiernan needed only that action to start him off. He barked an order, and in a moment his men were hurling their bombs, and the women shoppers, as well as the hooded lepers, were tearing at their eyes, retching, and milling helplessly about.

Kiernan's men slipped on the respirators which they always carried with tear gas equipment, and leaped down into the crowd. They were reluctant to touch those lepers, and they moved through the crowd awkwardly, unsure of themselves. Here and there, a leper, writhing under the effect of the gas, would barge into them, and they drew back hastily, fearful of contamination.

Wentworth shouted down at Kiernan, who had joined his men on the floor: "Slug them with your guns! Lay them out!" But his voice was drowned by the high-pitched screams of the women. No one heard him.

Swirls of the gas already were reaching the balcony, and Wentworth's eyes were beginning to smart. He saw the police moving around in uncertainty, and he looked around desperately for some means of getting their attention. His eyes lighted on a door in the balcony, marked: "Amplifier Room." This room would contain the controls of the system of loud speakers located at convenient spots throughout the building for the purpose of making special announcements to the shoppers.

He ran swiftly to that room, coughing from the irritation of the gas, which was coming on to the balcony in increasing quantities. He wrenched open the door and sprang inside, shutting it at once to keep out the gas.

The loudspeaker control panel and the microphone were rigged up at the far wall. Wentworth leaned against the door and stared for a moment at the three men who stood before

REIGN OF THE SNAKE MEN

The legless man seemed well able to protect himself.

55

that control panel. They were surely not the regular employees of the store! Their features were distinctly Asiatic, with high cheek bones and narrow, almost slit-like eyes, yellowish, parchment-like skins.

One of those three stood at the microphone. He was taller than the other two, and his pure white hair stood up in a straight pompadour from a high forehead. He had only one eye, and an old scar of a knife-blade across his left forehead and cheek, traversing the left optic, gave eloquent testimony as to how he had lost the sight of that eye. He wore no patch over it, and the empty socket stared out at Wentworth alongside the man's good eye, like the black muzzle of a wide-bored gun.

This man held a gun in his right hand, and as Wentworth appeared in the doorway, knives suddenly sprang into the hands of the other two. These two eyed him malevolently, their knives raised to hurl, holding the blades with their fingertips. Wentworth's quick glance swept over the room to a corner where lay two huddled bodies, wallowing in an ever-widening pool of blood. Those would be the regular control room operatives. They had met with short shrift at the hands of these three.

THE MAN at the microphone did not move as Wentworth entered, except that he kept his one good eye on him. With thin lips close to the microphone, he was speaking into it:

"Do not mind the tear gas, children of the Snake-master. Fight them, scratch them, claw them! Fight on for only a few minutes longer. The police are among you, and soon they will kill you all. Fight! Fight! Soon you will be dead, and our great master will remake you into healthy men with healthy bodies!"

Even as the one-eyed man spoke into the microphone, Wentworth could hear the dull booming amplification of his voice through the loudspeakers outside on the floor. The sound came to him through the door, together with the unearthly screams of the frightened shoppers. The man's words opened a new vista of comprehension for Wentworth. They explained why those lepers out there were so willing to die. Some one had promised them a new existence, a new incarnation, free from the pall of the disease that now festered in their bodies. Those lepers were nothing but dupes! Dupes of some master charlatan who used them for unholy ends!*

But he had no time for further concentration on this subject. These thoughts flashed through his mind in the seconds after he had closed the door behind him, and while the one-eyed man's

---

* Author's Note: Readers of previous novels will recall that Richard Wentworth had met the same kind of blind defiance to death in his past struggles with Tang-akhmut, the Living Pharaoh. There was no question in the Spider's mind but that Tang-akhmut possessed a tremendous degree of mental power by which he controlled the thoughts and emotions of human beings who served him. The Man from the East, as Wentworth had reason to know, possessed a great hidden lore of occult knowledge which was beyond the Occidental comprehension. Wentworth had seen servants of Tang-akhmut die cheerfully in the belief that their master was fully capable of bringing them back to life. He himself had witnessed that master's strange powers of hypnosis. And he feared and respected this enemy as he feared no other antagonist whom he had ever encountered in his career of unrelenting warfare against crime.

voice was raised in exhortation to the poor leprous dupes who were fighting his battle outside. But almost at the same instant, he was put on defensive. The two Asiatics had fallen into a crouch, raising the glistening knives in their yellow hands. As if at a signal, they both flipped their wrists, and the two keen-edged blades swished through the air silently, almost with the speed of bullets, directly at the Spider.

WENTWORTH HAD that faculty, peculiar to men who have lived hard, perilous lives, of thinking of several things at the same time, with different parts of his brain. Now, as he heard the one-eyed man's words, as a part of his mind concentrated on the purpose back of this raid, another portion of his consciousness had warned him of the deadly threat of those knives.

His own guns were empty, and he could not shoot the Asiatics; but almost in the instant that he read their purpose in their vicious eyes, he lunged forward in a crouching run that carried him toward the two by the sheer momentum of his body.

The knives whirred harmlessly over his head, and *spatted* into the door, hung there quivering. But Wentworth's lunge had already carried him into the nearest of the two yellow men.

His hunched shoulder caught the Asiatic in the groin, and the man was catapulted backward, uttering a thin yelp of pain, and crashed into the one-eyed announcer at the microphone. The two fell in a tangled mass on the floor, and Wentworth landed on all fours on the floor, pivoted on his hands, and straightened to meet the rush of the second Asiatic, who held another knife in a bony fist.

The man held it low, with the blade forward, like a butcher's knife, ready to rip upward into Wentworth's entrails in the deadly disemboweling thrust of Eastern knife-wielders. Yellow lips were twisted back from discolored teeth in a weird grin, of malignity.

Wentworth sidestepped with amazingly swift footwork as the yellow man lunged upward with the knife. The blade slipped along Wentworth's ribs, cutting through the cloth of his coat and grazing his skin on the left side. Wentworth clamped his left arm tight against his side, imprisoning the other's right arm, which had followed through with the lunge. Then the Spider's hard, bunched fist came up in a smashing blow to the knifeman's jaw, landed with a murderous thud and a sickening crunching of bone.

The attacker's head was snapped back as if on a spring, and the man seemed to collapse from within. Wentworth released his hold on the imprisoned arm, and its owner sank to the floor without a word, his jaw twisted at a queer, unnatural angle.

Wentworth heard a scraping sound behind him, and pivoted in time to see the one-eyed man slipping out through the door to the balcony. The Spider's first impulse was to chase the fugitive, but over the one-eyed man's shoulder he glimpsed the milling crowd in the store, saw that the police were making no headway against the fanatic leper men.

The latter were still mingling with the crowd, blinded, coughing, choking, but still clawing away at whatever came in their path. The uniformed men in the gas masks were pushing through the crowd, trying to get at the lepers, but they showed no great enthusiasm for getting at close quarters with the scabrous, half-naked men, whose scary chests bore the ugly design of the coiled cobra.

The police were hampered in the use of their guns because of the press of frantic shoppers who were also affected by the tear gas. The gas was spreading very thinly through the immense, air-conditioned floor, and its power was beginning to wear off. A few of the lepers had been struck down by the butts of police guns, but the rest still spread through the shrieking crowd.

All this Wentworth glimpsed through the open doorway, then the door slammed behind the retreating one-eyed man.

Wentworth leaped to the microphone, kicked at the hand of the groaning Asiatic whom he had butted in the groin, and who groveled on the floor in agony. Then the Spider brought his mouth close to the microphone, and pursed his lips, spoke suddenly in a voice that did not even faintly resemble his own. Wentworth's histrionic ability had been developed painstakingly, through years of arduous practice. So that now, as he sent his voice into the loudspeaker, it was the almost exact duplication of the voice of the one-eyed man!

"Children of the Snake-master!" he called. "Fight no longer! The time has come to die. The Snake-master wills it. Stand still, and let them shoot you down. The master promises that the sooner you die, the sooner shall he make you to live again!"

IT WAS a desperate attempt on Wentworth's part, and he had no way of telling whether the ruse had succeeded or not. He had gambled on the blind obedience of these dupes to the orders of their master. Would they obey?

Breathlessly, he raced to the door, flung it open. And a sigh of triumph escaped his taut lips. The ruse had worked!

All over the floor, the remaining leper men had ceased their mad, blind attack, and they now stood still, peering through smarting eyes at the police.

Captain Kiernan and his men appeared to be astounded at the sudden change in these mad attackers. They approached cautiously, bringing out handcuffs.

But the leper men began to utter screeches or rage at the sight of those shackles. The words that they shouted were in some strange foreign tongue, but their meaning was plain. They did not want to be taken prisoner; they wanted to be killed!

With mad, furious cries they leaped at the police, clawing, scratching, snatching at the gas masks, trying to tear them off so as to get at the officers' faces. They were deliberately provoking Kiernan's men to kill them! The police fell back before the mad onslaught, fearful of infection.

Wentworth shouted desperately: "Use your clubs! Use your gun butts! For God's sake, stop them. They can't harm you unless they scratch your skin. You're protected by gas masks. Slug them!"

Heartened by his words the police gained a new access of courage, and charged into the leper men, beating them down with gun butts and clubs. The lepers could not stand against the police once they had lost their fear of infection. In a few moments there were no more leper men left standing. The immediate peril was over.

But as Wentworth raced down from the balcony, the wailing and screaming of women rose in a high crescendo of terror from all points among the aisles. There were dozens of them who bore the marks of the leper men's raking nails across their cheeks, breasts and arms. All those women were infected with the loathsome bacillus of leprosy.

The victory belonged to the police—but the price was crushing. Dozens of homes would be thrown into despair tonight when it was learned that mothers, sisters, daughters, were in danger of becoming lepers.

And Wentworth caught a glimmering in that moment of what the Snake-master's real purpose must be. For he understood that the public would hereafter shun the department store of Fremont and Tynan like the plague.

NOW, HOWEVER, Wentworth was not thinking of that. With the felling of the last of the leper men, crowds from outside poured into the store to satisfy their curiosity as to what had occurred. People from the upper floors thronged downstairs by the escalators, and watched morbidly while the police moved about, gingerly handcuffing those of the half-naked leper men who were still alive but wounded.

White-coated interns from the ambulances which had arrived outside were pushing through the mulling crowd, trying to get to the wounded with first aid. Kiernan, ordinarily a highly efficient police officer, stood bewildered and uncertain as to what to do, while fear-crazed women who had been scratched by the bacilli-laden fingernails shrieked, swooned, or ran aimlessly about in frantic terror, tripping over prone bodies, interfering with the work of the interns and the dazed police.

Wentworth seized Kiernan by the arm, snapped: "Captain! You've got to clear the crowd out of here. But you've got to hold every person who has been scratched by the leper men. We can't allow them to roam the city. They might not spread infection, but they'd throw the whole populace into panic!"

Kiernan looked at him bewilderedly. His dazed glance failed to recognize Wentworth. "Wh-what kind of infection—"

"Leprosy, you fool!" Wentworth barked. "You must clear the store, and establish a cordon around it to hold all those in danger of infection. Snap into it, man!" He slapped the captain on the shoulder.

Kiernan sighed. "Hell, I'll do my best. I—I—this is a little beyond me. Say—" his eyes narrowed—"You look familiar—"

BUT WENTWORTH had already left him, and was approaching the ambulance interns working over the wounded leper men. To one of them he said crisply:

"There's something more important than that, doctor. You—"

The young intern frowned up at him. "More important? This man is badly wounded. He may die—"

Wentworth bent toward the intern, whispered softly: "You see that he is a leper, don't you?"

They had removed the wounded man's rubber mask, and it revealed a horribly pitted, scab-infected countenance.

"Of course I see. But I'm safe as long as I have no open wounds through which I can be infected—"

Wentworth took the intern's arm, pressed hard with his powerful fingers until he had swung him around to view the pandemonium of terrified women milling about on the floor.

"See those women? Dozens of them have open wounds—made by the fingernails of these men. They are all in danger of infection!"

The intern paled. "My God, I didn't know that. I—I—was outside in the ambulance, and I didn't really know what was going on here—"

"Now you know," Wentworth told him grimly. "Those women are all going to be held here until some quarantine facilities are prepared for receiving them. In the meantime, you must phone for drugs to inject. Perhaps a quick injection will check the infection. Phone for all available supplies of *sodium gynocardate*. You'll have to give all these women intravenous injections." He gave the young fellow a slight shove. "Go on, man, hurry."

The intern nodded dumbly. He did not know Wentworth, but he was impressed by his knowledge of the little-known drug that was used in cases of leprosy, and he was further impressed by Wentworth's poise and assurance. "I—I'll call every hospital in the neighborhood, sir, and have the labs get to work on turning out gynocardiac acid. We'll need phenol, too if we're going to inject—"

"Yes, yes!" Wentworth snapped. "Get going."

He watched the intern push through the crowd, and then made his way swiftly toward the balcony again. There was a short spiral stairway there, which led up to the mezzanine, and he had seen a face peering over the rail of the mezzanine—a face which he knew.

It was the darkly beautiful face of a woman. He had caught only a glimpse of her among the hundreds of fearful, peering faces of the people up there who had been watching the battle from the mezzanine; yet he would know it in a million.

He would never forget those dark eyes, seeming to look at the world from out of bottomless depths of inexplicable evil; those soft, inviting red lips that parted over sharp, white little pointed teeth, like the teeth of a vampire. It was a face that could attract a man irresistibly, even while he knew that its very attraction meant his doom.

Wentworth had hoped never to behold that face again. And as he raced up the spiral staircase, cold clamps seemed to contract his heart, and his blood chilled with the certainty of the desperate battle that he was now sure the ensuing days would bring.

For he knew now, without a doubt, that he was pitted against the cleverest, the most unscrupulous and the most ruthless force of evil that had ever been spawned upon the earth. That face he had glimpsed on the balcony was the face of the Princess Issoris—the sister of Tang-akhmut, the Living Pharaoh, the Spider's deadliest enemy, and the arch-enemy of civilization!

ONE THING was certain—wherever Issoris was, Tang-akhmut would not be far away. The sight of Issoris, coupled with the fantastic atrocity that was occurring here, was definite proof that the sinister Living Pharaoh was making another bid to master the city.

On the main floor, more police had arrived, including several high officials from headquarters. But Wentworth paid them no attention as he raced up the spiral staircase, and swung onto the broad floor of the mezzanine.

Here, hundreds of people lined the railing, peering down at

the scene of terror below. The mad assault of the leper men had been confined to the main floor, and these people, though free from personal injury or danger, were nevertheless shocked into stunned silence by the nightmare that was taking place under their eyes.

Wentworth gazed about eagerly, for sight of the woman, Issoris. She had apparently left her place at the railing, for she was not there.

Suddenly, he spotted her smartly tailored figure. She was just passing through a doorway into an office at the rear of the mezzanine. Just as Wentworth sighted her, the door closed behind her. The austere lettering on that door now faced him:

JOHN T. TYNAN
Vice-President

Wentworth pushed through the crowd toward that door, while insistent questions pounded at his brain. What was the sister of Tang-akhmut doing in the office of the vice-president of Fremont and Tynan? Was Tynan destined for the same fate as that which had been met by Lawrence Fremont?

Had Issoris seen him, as he had seen her? There could be little doubt that she had. If so, was she truly fleeing from him, or was she leading him into a trap?

The sister of Tang-akhmut was a clever, ruthless woman, made doubly dangerous by the sheer beauty with which she had been endowed. Also, she knew Wentworth well enough from past encounters, to understand that once he saw her he would follow her inexorably, no matter what the odds.

It had taken Wentworth precious minutes to push through the throng on the main floor, and to mount the spiral staircase. If she had wished, Issoris could easily have made her escape. Had she deliberately timed her movements so that he could see her entering Tynan's office—certain that he would never hesitate to follow?

Wentworth was close to the door now. His guns were empty again, but he did not pause to reload them. If a trap lay beyond that door, he must face it—with or without guns. But he must not give the clever Issoris an extra moment's breathing space.

Firmly, he put his hand on the knob, twisted, and thrust open the door....

CHAPTER 5
THE LEGLESS ONE

LESS THAN ten blocks away from the Fremont and Tynan Department Store, Nita van Sloan sat anxiously at the window of her superbly furnished modernistic living room on the third floor of the Northern Arms Apartments, overlooking Central Park. Her features, revealed in the last dull light of the late afternoon, were markedly patrician, from the straight, small nose to the long curve of her white throat.

She was peering out of the window, across the angle of the southern edge of Central Park, toward where she could see the tall lines of the Fremont and Tynan Building rising above the other structures on Fifth Avenue. Born on fitful breezes, there had come to her from that direction the sounds of shooting;

and after that the clang of ambulances and the wailing sirens of police cars.

With a slim hand pressed at her throat, she swung away from the window, and spoke to the tall, bearded man who stood just behind her.

"Ram Singh! You should have gone with Mr. Wentworth. I—I am sure he is in danger. You know how I feel those things. Something is going on over there at Fremont and Tynan's. You can hear the shooting. And Dick—Mr. Wentworth—is in the thick of it!"

Ram Singh stirred uncomfortably. He was leaning heavily on a cane held in his right hand, and it was apparent that his right leg was a bit stiff. White teeth gleamed through his black beard as he spoke in a low voice.

"I, too, fear for the master, *memsahib*. But I must obey him in this as in all else. He feared danger for you, just as you fear it for him!"

Ram Singh, as he stood in the half light of the living room, was a powerful figure of a man. Corded muscles stood out on his neck, and the cloth of his coat rippled over the muscles of his back and shoulders. In strange contrast to the dark blue, double-breasted suit he wore was the silken turban wound about his head, and the long, carefully trimmed beard that covered most of his face.

Ram Singh was a Sikh of purest blood, proud of his caste, who could trace his ancestry back to Nanak Shah, the sixteenth-century founder of the Sikh nation in India. With blood in his veins that was the equal of any reigning monarch in the world,

Nita struggled in the grip of two cobra-branded men.

this descendant of a race of warriors found happiness and satisfaction in serving Richard Wentworth; and no one was more devoted to him than this fierce Punjab warrior—except, perhaps, Wentworth's fiancée, Nita van Sloan. Not so long ago, Ram Singh had been wounded in a pitched battle with a small army of Tang-akhmut's followers.

It was on that occasion that Tang-akhmut and his cohorts had been badly beaten, and Tang-akhmut and his sister, Issoris, had barely escaped with their lives. Ram Singh's stiff leg was a result of that encounter.

Now, his ears pricked up as the sounds of continued shooting trickled up to them, and his nostrils flared, like a bloodhound closing in on a stag. His fingers played with the haft of the long knife in the sheath under his belt. He had moved up close beside Nita van Sloan, and was looking down into the street below. His eyes burned with sudden fierce joy.

"Memsahib," he said softly, "there is much fighting there on the other side of the park, and I was fretful to remain in idleness. But I think that now we shall have our own share of excitement. The master was right in keeping me here!" He directed Nita's glance to the strange figure that had appeared out of the Park, across the street from the house.

Nita uttered a little gasp, and leaned forward. What—she saw caused her to shudder in revulsion. The man who had come out of the park wore a pair of wide white pantaloons, and a short vest of white silk material. Under the vest showed swarthy, hairy skin. His torso was bare except for that vest, and on his chest there could plainly be discerned a queer design that looked, from where Nita sat, like a red circle within which was the coiled figure of a snake of some sort. The man wore a white skull cap, to which were attached flaps that came down over his ears and fastened under his chin.

But aside from the man's outlandish costume, the thing that shocked Nita into startled wonder was *the live snake coiled about his neck!*

THE REPTILE'S long coils seemed to be alive with sinuous energy, and its ugly little head poked straight upward in front of its owner. Both the man's hands were occupied, holding a long flute upon which he was playing a mournful, wailing dirge. And the snake's coils undulated to the fantastic tune, in slow time to the tempo of the music, while its wicked head remained immovable.

Ram Singh's breath came in a hiss through clenched teeth. *"Memsahib!* It is a fakir from the east—a snake-charmer. He is an evil man. Where he walks, no good can survive!"

The snake-charmer came to a stop at the curb, directly opposite the entrance of the Northern Arms, and he continued to play his weird tune on the flute, while the reptile around his neck kept time to it. Pedestrians halted, amazed, not knowing whether to be amused or frightened. Many strange sights appear in the streets of a cosmopolitan city like New York, but this was the strangest they had witnessed outside a circus sideshow. Rendered nervous by the sounds of shooting and sirens from the direction of Fifth Avenue, pedestrians gave the weird snake-charmer a wide berth, many of them crossing the street to avoid passing near him.

THE SPIDER

A policeman at the corner started toward the outlandishly garbed snake-man. The officer walked purposefully, with a frown. He was annoyed that a nuisance like this should turn up on his ordinarily quiet beat. He didn't know whether to run the man in, or shoo him away. No doubt he was a peddler of some sort, come to sell his wares here. Well, he'd soon know that Central Park West was no place to pull any stunts like that!

It was just at this moment, while the cop was hurrying down the street toward the snake-man, that a taxicab swung into Central Park West from the side street, and screeched to a stop in front of the entrance of the Northern Arms. Its door was flung open, and a strange, misshapen being climbed out to the street.

Nita and Ram Singh, watching from the upper window, leaned forward tensely to get a better view. Nita exclaimed with a sudden rush of pity: "Oh, the poor man!"

The being that had emerged from the taxicab was doubtless a man. But his appearance was enough to arouse the sentiment of pity in the breast of anyone beholding him. Both legs were gone at the knees, and he wobbled on the short padded stumps in awkward, ungainly fashion, half supporting himself with his right hand which touched the pavement. Left hand there was none. The left arm seemed to have been sheared off close to the shoulder, and the short coat had been made with only one sleeve. But the thing that sent a shudder through Nita's slender frame was the relative size of the unfortunate being's head and torso. For his head was wide at the top, entirely bald, and almost as big as the rest of his foreshortened body.

But now, Nita and Ram Singh had no time to indulge in pity.

For things began to happen down there with devastating swiftness. No sooner had the legless man reached the curb than he began to amble awkwardly toward the entrance to Nita's apartment house. And at once the flute of the snake-charmer across the street began to emit loud, strident, high-pitched notes.

As if at a signal, dark shadows detached themselves from the shadows of the park, resolved themselves into figures of half-naked men, with knives glistening in their hands. There were perhaps a dozen of them, and they all ran directly toward the legless man. Two of them crouched in the street, raised their knives and sent them hurtling through the air at him.

THE LEGLESS man, for all his disability, seemed well able to defend himself. A gun had appeared in his single hand, and it barked once, twice. The two who had been about to throw their knives toppled to the ground with blood spurting from their chests—chests upon which were emblazoned the symbol of the red circle and the coiled cobra. Now the others were closing in on the legless man, and he emptied his gun at them, stopping them for an instant.

Then he turned, and ran in shuffling, ludicrous fashion, into the apartment house. After him came the surviving knife-men.

The echoes of the legless man's shots were still reverberating thunderously through the street. And on the opposite side, another little drama was being played to its bitter conclusion. The policeman who had approached the snake-charmer there had swung about in sudden alarm as the knife-men emerged from the shadows of the park. As his widening eyes glimpsed the situation, he reached frantically for his revolver.

But the snake-man, feverishly playing the flute, moved a step closer, and the ugly snake on his shoulder darted out its ugly head at the policeman in a lightning swoop that struck with a vicious snap at the policeman's exposed neck, just above the collar. The policeman clapped his hand to his neck, dropping the gun in sudden agony. He screamed, and his voice rose above the shots of the legless man's gun. Then, just as the legless man disappeared into Nita's house, the policeman twisted into a heap of searing anguish, slumping to the sidewalk and rolling over in a paroxysm. Suddenly he stiffened, and stretched out at full length. His fingers clawed open and shut spasmodically, and then became rigid. He was dead.

Nita leaned far out the window, wide-eyed, gripping the long-barreled Colt's .45 which she had snatched from a drawer of her writing desk, and which she never kept far from her these days. Her gaze was focused on the pitiable figure of the dead patrolman, and a spasm of horror crossed her face. She had never seen a man die so fast from the bite of a cobra. This must be some new, little-known species of the cobra family, as deadly as its master.

The snake-charmer had abruptly ceased playing his odious tune, and had started back toward the park. Pedestrians were running wildly in aimless panic, seeking shelter from the sudden battle that had swept over the street Nita's little mouth was set in a tight line as she sighted the Colt's down at the disappearing snake-charmer. She fired three times in quick succession, and could have sworn she hit the man. But he disappeared into the shadows of the park. If the snake-charmer had been hit, he could not be seriously wounded, for it had not stopped him. The two wounded knife-men in the street also crept away into the shelter of the park.

Nita pulled her head in from the window, exclaiming: "Ram Singh! That legless man must be trying to get to us! Go and help—"

She stopped short. Ram Singh was gone. Slowly, Nita van Sloan smiled. Ram Singh needed no instructions from her. He had already gone to the aid of the legless man, who must be fighting for his life downstairs in the lobby....

RAM SINGH had slipped out of the apartment almost at the first shots of the legless man. The huge Sikh's eyes were gleaming with the prospect of battle as he descended in the self-service elevator, and slid open the door of the cage at the street floor. He barged out into the lobby, and his quick eyes took in the scene at a glance.

The deformed man had retreated into the lobby, and was fighting desperately to defend himself against the attack of the surviving three knife-men. They were coming at him from all sides, their knives describing vicious arcs as they lunged and struck. The deformed man was smashing at them with his clubbed revolver, swinging it with his one long, simian-like arm. Sweat stood out on his high forehead, and on the great expanse of his bald dome. Near the door lay the bloody body of the Northern Arms doorman. A knife hilt protruded from his throat, attesting to the ruthlessness of the knife-men.

When Ram Singh appeared, the three knife-wielders turned upon him like wildcats upon a great bear, surging toward the big Sikh with knives flashing. The legless man slumped down, exhausted from his desperate resistance; in another moment he would have succumbed to the attack. Ram Singh's appearance had apparently saved him.

Now, as the three little Asiatics swarmed toward him, Ram Singh's white teeth gleamed in a smile of pure, ferocious joy, and his own long-bladed knife leaped into his hand. *"Wah!"* he shouted. "Come, jackals! Come and fight a *man!*"

The red circles with the insignia of the coiled cobra gleamed blood-red upon the chests of the three Asiatics as they rushed at him. Ram Singh's knife flashed in and out, parrying, lunging, thrusting, slashing. His great body stood firm as a rock, never yielding an inch even when knives grazed him, even when points flashed in his face.

His blade seemed to be everywhere, slithering against the attackers' knives, drawing sparks of fire from the striking metal. He slashed downward at an angle, viciously, and a man screamed, fell away with a deep gash in his neck from which blood spurted like a fountain.

Ram Singh laughed loud, in joyous lust of battle. "Well, jackal, did you relish the taste of my blade?"

The remaining two increased the fury of their attack. They did not seem to fear death; their only purpose seemed to be to cut down Ram Singh. One of them remained at close quarters, engaging Ram Singh's blade, while the other backed away, dropped to one knee and poised his knife in the air, waiting for a chance to throw it. The other tried to turn in such fashion as to expose Ram Singh's back to that poised knife.

THE WARY Sikh sensed their purpose and suddenly dropped to one knee, lunged upward with his weapon. The blade caught the Asiatic in the groin, and snapped. The Asiatic screamed, and called to his fellow in a foreign tongue. The kneeling man drew back his hand to throw the knife.

And Ram Singh, with a deep laugh rumbling in his chest, stepped close to the man he had wounded in the groin, lifted him from the floor like a child, and hurled him full at the kneeling Asiatic!

The kneeling man threw the knife just at that moment, and it struck into the body of his fellow, hurtling through the air. Then the screaming man in the air landed against his fellow. There was a thud, and the sound of cracking bone, and the two hit the floor together, lay still. The Asiatic who had thrown the knife lay with his skull cracked open. Both were dead.

Ram Singh laughed again, and swung toward the deformed man, who was wiping sweat from his forehead with the single sleeve of his coat. Ram Singh boomed: "Well, thou one-limbed one, I have saved thee from death. What is thy name?"

The tremendously disproportioned head of the one-armed, legless man reached barely to Ram Singh's waist. His broad, misshapen face was twisted into a gargoyle of laughter, but his eyes gleamed with an intelligence that almost awed Ram Singh. It was as if the man were compensated for his deformity by having been endowed with the mind of a superman.

"Ho, my brave Sikh!" he said ironically. "Thou hast done well. Thy muscles are good, even if thy brain is weak!"

Ram Singh frowned threateningly. "Quiet, thou spawn of the

devil. Do you mock me after I have preserved thy life? Quiet, or I will choke the life out of thee!" He bent forward, stretching his big hands toward the cripple's neck.

The other laughed up at him tauntingly. "Good, my brave Sikh! Throttle me. I have been cursed enough by Allah. Death has no terrors for me. Come, use those big hands of yours!"

Ram Singh muttered to himself, then spoke aloud, less angrily: "It would be an ill act of mine to take the life of an unfortunate such as thou. Yet I will show thee how easily I could do it" Suddenly he bent down, seized the deformed body in his great arms, and lifted the man up to his shoulder. "Watch thy tongue, thou misbegotten son of Shaitan, or I will dash thee to the floor. Now quick—by what name do men know thee?"

The cripple seemed quite comfortable on Ram Singh's shoulder. But he glanced uneasily toward the street, from where could be heard the cries of excited people, and the shrilling of police whistles.

"Soon the police will be here. You are Ram Singh, the servant of Wentworth *sahib*, and of the beautiful *memsahib*, Nita van Sloan. I am known in Punjabi as Chenab Sind. I have risked much, as you have seen, to come here to speak with your mistress. Take me quickly to her, so that I can give her my message before the police come!"

Ram Singh still held the man high, looked at him suspiciously. "You have a message for my mistress? Then give it to me, and I will tell her."

Chenab Sind laughed raucously. "No. I do not deal with servants, my Sikh!"

78

Ram Singh's face reddened, and he seemed on the point of letting the deformed creature drop to the floor. But he mastered his anger, said: "Good. I will take thee to her. But if thou shouldst try any kind of trick while in her presence, I will snuff out thy life as I would a toad's!"

Chenab Sind said nothing, but looked at him unblinkingly. RAM SINGH heard the patter of feet outside. That must be the police. He hurried into the elevator, set the man down and picked up his cane, which he had dropped there. Then he sent the cage sliding up to the third floor. He made the cripple precede him to Nita's door. It was closed and locked. Ram Singh muttered an oath, and rattled the knob, while Chenab Sind watched him sardonically.

Ram Singh pressed his finger hard on the bell, heard it ring within the apartment. There was no answer, but almost at once, two quick shots thundered from somewhere on the other side of the door. Then Nita's voice: "Ram Singh! Help! The—"

Her voice was cut off with a gurgle, and Ram Singh beat frantically at the heavy door without effect. Suddenly he snapped: "The service entrance!" He swung about, fairly leaped over Chenab Sind, and hurled himself through the hall door to the service corridor. The service door of the apartment was wide open, and just within it Nita van Sloan was struggling in the grip of two half-naked cobra-branded men.

One of them had a cruel hand clamped over her mouth, and was twisting her still smoking revolver out of her hand, while the other was about to strike her on the temple with the reversed handle of his knife. Their intention had been, no doubt, to stun

79

her and spirit her down through the service exit in the basement, which opened on the side street.

Beyond them, Ram Singh could see two more of the Asiatics sprawled on the floor where Nita's first two shots had hurled them. Nita was kicking out at her assailants spiritedly with her feet, and trying frantically to avoid the butt of the knife. Her eyes, wide with anger and the excitement of the fray, betrayed no fear.

Ram Singh was unarmed, for he had cast away the broken knife. He had, however, his cane; and this he raised in the air, uttered a low, rumbling cry of rage, and launched himself at the group.

The flailing cane swished viciously through the air, and smashed into the upraised wrist of the yellow man who held the knife. The wrist snapped with a sickening crunch, the man squealed, and stumbled away. The other took his hand from Nita's mouth, leaped to one side, and whipped out a knife. He raised this to hurl at Ram Singh, his small eyes gleaming with spiteful hate.

Ram Singh was ten feet away from the man, and that knife could travel through the air with the speed of light once it left the Asiatic's hand. These men were masters of the art of hurling a knife, and could probably send it into a mark as accurately as a westerner could shoot. Ram Singh was handicapped by his game leg, and could not duck or sidestep quickly enough to dodge the murderous weapon. He had nothing with which to protect his body against the keen blade.

In that split second of time while the shining knife was poised in the Asiatic's hand, Ram Singh saw death staring him in the face. Yet he did not flinch.

His deep-throated roar of battle rang through the hall, and he leaped directly at the other. The Asiatic's hand was already descending in that wide arc that would send the knife spinning at him, and in an instant the keen point would bite into Ram Singh's flesh.

But Ram Singh was a human bull-dog. His creed was to fight as long as breath remained in his body. He would defend Nita until he could no longer lift a hand. Even if the knife were to strike a mortal spot, he wanted to get his hands on that Asiatic's throat—on the throat of a man who dared to attack his beloved Nita.

THAT KNIFE never left the Asiatic's hand. For Nita van Sloan still held her revolver, which the man with the broken wrist had abandoned to her. She snapped it up, pulled the trigger frantically, and the thunderous report reverberated through the room and the corridor as the heavy slug caught the Asiatic in the side of the head. The yellow man's skull was smashed in by the heavy caliber bullet, and his face seemed to disintegrate. The knife dropped from nerveless fingers, and the man's already dead body crumpled to the floor.

The man with the broken wrist fled as Ram Singh lurched toward him. He leaped across the bodies of his two companions, whom Nita had shot, and reached the window only a second before

Ram Singh. The fellow's face was twisted with the pain of his wrist.

Ram Singh shouted: "Fool! You cannot escape that way—"

The big Sikh broke off with an ejaculation of amazement mingled with stark unbelief. The Asiatic was not seeking safety. He was seeking death!

Before Ram Singh could reach him, he had vaulted the window sill, and threw himself headlong out into the air. His body spun dizzily, and then crashed into the pavement below with a sickening thud. Ram Singh peered down dourly, at the battered object that had just now been a living man. The fellow had failed in his attempt to kidnap Nita, and he had preferred death to facing his master.

Down below, a crowd had gathered about the suicide. A police prowl car was at the door, empty. The police from that car were doubtless already in the lobby of the building, puzzling over the murdered body of the doorman. Ram Singh drew in his head, turned back into the room. He saw Nita standing with her revolver, facing the misshapen, crippled Chenab Sind, who had ambled awkwardly into the room.

Nita was breathing hard, her breasts rising and falling quickly. "Who are you?" she demanded of the legless man.

Chenab Sind stood just inside the doorway, his long left hand almost touching the dead Asiatic whom Nita had shot in the head; but he seemed to pay no attention to the corpse. His small eyes peered up at Nita from his oversized face.

"I am Chenab Sind," he said, speaking slowly and carefully in English, but without trace of accent. "You are Nita van Sloan, the woman of Richard Wentworth."

He said it without inflection, more as a statement than a

question. Ram Singh frowned, hurried to Nita's side. "We have no time to talk," he urged her. "Those oxen of the police will be here at once. Let us go away from here."

Nita raised a hand to silence him. She did not take her eyes from Chenab Sind. "What do you want here?" she asked the legless man.

Chenab Sind chuckled. "I came here to warn you against a powerful enemy of your friend, Wentworth. You are impatient with me—but you shall not be impatient when I have mentioned that enemy's name."

"Well, go on," Nita snapped. "Unless you want to stay here and be held by the police when they come."

"No, lady, I do not wish to be held by the police. But we have time. They do not know what floor to search first. Let me tell you the name of the enemy. It is—Tang-akhmut!"

Nita breathed even faster. "What of Tang-akhmut?"

"He is back. With a terror that your city will not be able to withstand. He brings a plague of the east to spread in your city; the plague of leprosy. And he brings knife-men like these, whom your Sikh has just routed. You know that Wentworth received a telephone call a short while ago, warning him that there would be trouble at the store of Fremont and Tynan?"

"Yes." Nita looked at him queerly. "I was with Dick when he got the call. It was true. I could hear shooting from that direction, just before you arrived."

Chenab Sind nodded that huge head of his. "It was I who warned him. I come to offer you alliance—you and Wentworth. Look at me. I am a poor creature without legs, lacking an arm.

And what I am, Tang-akhmut has made me." The cripple's face was suddenly contorted with passion. "I have reason to hate the one who calls himself the Living Pharaoh. And I wish to prevent him from doing to others as he has done to me. Let me join you!"

NITA LOOKED questionably at Ram Singh, who shrugged. "I do not trust this one-limbed spawn of Shaitan. But it is not for me to judge. Let us take him to Wentworth *sahib*. Let the master decide."

Nita nodded quickly. "I'm going to take a chance. Mr. Wentworth and I have a prearranged meeting place in the event of trouble. He will go there when he leaves Fremont and Tynan's—" there was a sudden catch in her voice, which she smothered bravely—"if—if nothing has happened to him there. Come. Let's go before the police get here!"

She led the way through the apartment into the kitchen. Here, a closet opened into a corridor that led into the adjoining building, where there was another apartment, almost a duplicate of the one they had left. Nita owned both of these buildings, the second one having its entrance on the side street. She had had this connecting corridor built especially for the purpose of affording a means of escape in case she or Wentworth should be hard-pressed. Nita felt regretfully that she would have to abandon this retreat after today. By some uncanny means, it had become known to too many people, and now when the police found the dead bodies of the Asiatics, it would be sealed to her and Wentworth.

As they descended in the service elevator to the basement exit, Ram Singh was careful to remain always between the legless man and Nita, not allowing him to touch her. His suspicions were not yet allayed.

Nita explained swiftly that after Ram Singh had left, she had heard a knock at the service entrance of the apartment, and, thinking it was the Sikh returning, had opened the door without ascertaining who was there. The Asiatics had thrust in, and Nita had fled back into the living room, and picked up the Colt which she had put down after shooting at the snake-charmer. She had killed two of them, but a third had come up behind her, and it was then that she had shouted for Ram Singh.

Chenab Sind nodded. "They planned to seize you," he told her. "I knew of that plot, and came at once. But Vara-Kun—the snake-charmer whom you saw from your window—was quicker than I."

Ram Singh asked him suspiciously: "Who are you, one-limbed one, that you know of the plans of Tang-akhmut?"

Chenab Sind smiled tantalizingly. "I will explain all when we meet Wentworth!"

In the basement of the apartment house there was an exit to a garage in the rear, where two cars were parked, ready for instant use. One was Nita's coupé, the other a sedan. Nita's eyes flashed with sudden determination.

"Ram Singh," she exclaimed, "I am not going with you. You take this man to the place you know of. I shall go in the coupé to Fremont and Tynan's. I—feel that Dick is in need of me!"

Ram Singh started to protest, but she stopped him imperiously. "Do as I say!" she snapped. "Am I a child to be ordered around, and wet-nursed by a bearded guardian? Stand out of my way!"

Speechless, poor Ram Singh allowed her to get into the coupé and drive out of the garage. Then, frowning under the sardonic gaze of the cripple, he lifted Chenab Sind into the sedan, and drove out after her. Her coupé had already passed out of sight. Ram Singh could not have known what far-reaching consequences that willful action of Nita's would bring about. Had he guessed them, he would have stopped her by main force....

CHAPTER 6
A TRAP FOR A SPIDER

AT THE exact time when Nita, Ram Singh and Chenab Sind were descending in the service elevator of the adjoining apartment house, Richard Wentworth, ten blocks away, had his hand on the knob of the executive office door of the vice-president of Fremont and Tynan.

He was certain that in a few moments, when Captain Kiernan had recovered from his bewilderment at the strange events of the raid of the leper men, the captain would suddenly remember that Richard Wentworth was in the building and was wanted for murder. He would have the place fine-combed in search for him.

And Wentworth himself had suggested that a cordon be placed around the store. If the Spider was to escape so that he could be free to fight this new menace which Tang-akhmut had brought to overshadow the city, he must escape now—before the cordon was completed.

But Wentworth could not have been dragged out of that store with a team of horses after glimpsing the dark, evilly beautiful countenance of Issoris. He had to investigate her presence here at once; and the matter of getting away could be faced later.

He thrust open the door, stepped swiftly inside and closed it behind him, standing with his back to it. His cool, gray eyes snapped around the room, wary of a trap. But there was no trap in evidence.

John T. Tynan, vice-president of Fremont and Tynan, sat behind the broad, expensive mahogany desk against the window. He had both hands on the glass top of the desk, and was in the act of rising. Tynan's usually ruddy face was a bit pale, and the tip of his tongue was nervously licking his thin lips. Otherwise, there was little to show that he had been seriously affected by the dreadful events that had taken place on the main floor of his store.

The Princess Issoris was standing halfway between the door and the desk, half turned to face Wentworth as he barged into the room. Her hands clasped tightly a green purse which matched the deep green dress visible under her sable coat. Her face was collected, cool, almost expressionless; yet her eyes were tinged with a slight hint of vindictive triumph as she gazed steadily at Wentworth.

Wentworth smiled tightly. Tynan spoke in quick, nervous fashion. "W-who are you? What do you mean by breaking in—"

Issoris laughed. "It's all right, John. The gentleman looks quite respectable. I think he's harmless."

Wentworth's eyes rested broodingly on her. "Thank you, madam. I had not expected to see you so soon—again."

Her face assumed a blank expression. "So soon? I don't understand. Have we met before?"

"Indeed we have," Wentworth assured her. "Surely your memory cannot be so poor! Recall if you please, a certain night when I, with some friends of mine, raided the hideout of your—er—redoubtable brother, Tang-akhmut—"

He was interrupted by the pushing open of the door behind him. Captain Kiernan stood there, with a plain-clothes man behind him. Kiernan had a gun in his hand.

"Richard Wentworth," he barked, "I arrest you for murder! Put up your hands!"

The captain's face was pallid, and his eyes seemed to mirror the horror of the things that had just happened on the floor of the store. He repeated ominously: "For murder, Wentworth—*and* worse! For inciting lepers to riot, for spreading leprosy in the city, for causing innocent women to get the disease. God! And you stood out there, right next to me, while those lepers clawed and fought my men! *Get your hands up, or by God, I'll drill you!*"

WENTWORTH'S EYES narrowed. He understood now the trap that had been laid for him by the beautiful, dangerously clever sister of Tang-akhmut, who was watching him now with a faintly ironic smile curving her soft red lips. He faced Kiernan tautly.

"You're mad!" he said in a low, tense voice. "I was trying to help you. People outside will tell you that I fought those lepers

Wentworth ran with his burden to the subway entrance.

in the street. You yourself heard me order them to stop fighting over the loudspeakers—"

Kiernan was shaking his head in disbelief. "That wasn't your voice on the loudspeakers, Wentworth. And as for shooting down the lepers—" his voice was bitter—"you don't give a damn about them anyway. Didn't you order them to fight until they were killed? I heard you myself—"

Wentworth interrupted impatiently. "I won't try to convince you now, Kiernan. You're too bullet-headed. But you'll at least believe this." He gestured toward the svelte figure of Issoris. *"That woman is the Princess Issoris, the sister of Tang-akhmut, the man whom I helped you to drive from the city!* Doesn't her presence here mean anything to you? Don't you understand that Tang-akhmut is back? Don't you—"

He stopped as the brittle, amused laughter of Issoris broke in on his impassioned words.

"My dear man!" Issoris exclaimed. "Whoever you are, you are either mad, or a very clever rogue." She smiled at Kiernan, who was looking at her curiously. "Of course, Captain, the things this man says are fantastic. Mr. Tynan here—" she went around the desk and put a hand on the shoulder of John T. Tynan—"will tell you who I am—that is, if you need any proof to refute this wild accusation!"

Tynan nodded nervously. He licked his lips, looked from Wentworth to Kiernan, then spoke slowly, exploding his bombshell into the room: "This lady, captain, is not what the gentleman accuses her of being. She is—my wife!"

90

Wentworth's face flushed a dull red. He walked slowly toward the desk, utterly oblivious of the threat of Kiernan's revolver.

"Tynan," he said tightly, through set lips, "you are doing a terrible thing. Your partner is lying murdered outside in the street. Leprosy is being spread among the shoppers in your store, and will soon be rife in the city; yet you stand there and protect the sister of the man who is responsible for it all—you even give her your name. Think well, Tynan, before you commit yourself. Admit that this woman isn't your wife. Some one is forcing you to do this. Believe me, Tynan, it would be better for you and for the city if you admitted everything—before it's too late!"

Tynan's eyes lowered before the boring gaze of Richard Wentworth, "Damn it!" he exclaimed stubbornly, "I order you to stop insulting my wife! I won't have it!"

Kiernan's harsh voice rasped: "That'll be enough of this comedy! Come on, Wentworth. Your jig is up—"

Wentworth understood when he was licked. He could do no further good here. The cards were stacked too well and too cleverly against him—and against the city. His only chance to fight the swiftly tightening meshes of this insidious web that was being woven about him was to retain his freedom, to gain a breathing spell to plan a campaign of defense. That chance at freedom he had deliberately sacrificed when he came up here to Tynan's office. Now he must extricate himself. Even while Tynan was speaking, he had grasped the hopelessness of selling his innocence to the stubborn, conscientious Kiernan. And his quick mind sent his perfectly coördinated body into action before the captain had finished talking.

HE STRUCK back violently with his left elbow, catching the muzzle of Kiernan's gun and deflecting it. The gun exploded with a deafening blast and the slug went wild, ripped into the wall. At the same time, Wentworth leaped around the desk, seized Tynan by the coat collar, and twisted the vice-president's right arm behind him in a punishing hammerlock. He swung Tynan about as shield between himself and the guns of Kiernan and the plainclothes detective, who was still at the door. Kiernan had been about to fire again, but he held his finger on the trigger as he saw that Tynan's body intervened between himself and his target.

Tynan cried out hoarsely in agony as his arm came within an ace of snapping. He dared not resist as Wentworth drew him backward toward the side door of the office. Kiernan started to run around the desk to get at them, and Issoris shrieked: "Shoot! Shoot! Don't let him escape!"

Kiernan was upon them now, his gun raised to strike at the Spider past Tynan's head. Wentworth's back was to the closed side door. He raised his right foot, thrust straight out with it past his prisoner. His foot caught Kiernan in the abdomen, sent him violently backward. He collided with the plainclothes man, who was crossing the room to his assistance, and the two of them crashed to the floor.

The face of the Princess Issoris was transformed with fury, and she was fumbling frantically in her handbag for a gun. But before she could get it out, Wentworth had slipped through the side door, slammed it shut. He retained his grip on the feebly struggling Tynan, and glanced around the room he had entered.

He was in an office evidently used by Tynan's secretary and typists. It was vacant now, for its occupants were no doubt on the mezzanine, watching the scene on the main floor.

Some one pounded at the side door, but Wentworth had slipped the catch, and it was locked. Tynan gasped: "My arm! God, don't break it!"

Wentworth scowled, swung Tynan around, let go of the man's arm, and brought a swift uppercut up to his jaw. Tynan's breath was expelled in a gasp, and he wilted. Wentworth caught him before he fell to the floor, and heaved his unconscious form over his shoulder. Then he made for the outer door, stepped out onto the mezzanine with his burden effectively screening his face from the crowd there. No one paid him any attention, for they were all avidly watching the milling crowd on the main floor, where terror-stricken women impeded the work of the police and interns.

WENTWORTH RAN swiftly along the mezzanine and turned the corner of the corridor just as the door of Tynan's office burst open and Kiernan came barging out. Wentworth, glancing back over his shoulder, saw Kiernan leap toward the door of the room he had just quit. Luckily, the captain had not looked down along the mezzanine floor, else he might have spotted the Spider and his burden. As it was, Wentworth was unmolested as he found another staircase and made his way down to the main floor.

Police guards were stationed at all the doors, and it would be impossible for him to get past them. Tynan's body was beginning to grow heavy. In a matter of moments Captain Kiernan would be out, and would give the alarm. The police would close in on Wentworth.

But it was characteristic of him that he did not attempt to save himself alone. Up there in the office he had decided that he must question Tynan at his leisure, must extract from the man the secret of his knowledge. Wentworth did not doubt that Tynan must know something about the raid—else why had he offered the protection of his name to Issoris? If he could only get the unconscious vice-president away from here, he would be able to extract valuable information from him.

Wentworth's questing eyes spotted the open door of a rest room, which had been converted into a first aid room. An intern in a white coat was in there, bending over one of the wounded lepers who were lying on a stretcher.

The Spider's eyes lighted with sudden inspiration. He carried Tynan through the milling crowd, shouldering past hurrying police who did not even give him a second glance. In the rest room, the intern looked up from his patient as Wentworth deposited Tynan's form on the floor. The intern's white coat sleeve bore the inscription: *"Mercy Hospital."* He was a young fellow, and he suspected nothing as Wentworth stepped close to him.

"I hate to do this, young man," Wentworth told him, "but it's a hell of an emergency!"

And he brought up his fist in a swift arc that caught the intern squarely on the point of the jaw. The intern's head snapped back, his eyes rolled up, and Wentworth eased him down to the floor; then without pausing, he stripped off his own coat, donned the intern's white uniform jacket. He dragged the intern over to a corner, came back and rolled the unconscious, wounded leper off the stretcher and placed Tynan on it.

He could hear Kiernan shouting somewhere up in the mezzanine, hoarsely bellowing orders to search everywhere for Richard Wentworth. "Shoot on sight!" Kiernan ordered. "Don't let that man escape!"

Wentworth smiled thinly, and stepped out of the rest room, looking for all the world like one of the callow young ambulance interns. He spotted an ambulance driver passing, made sure that the man was not from the Mercy Hospital, and called to him urgently. The driver came over, and Wentworth exclaimed: "Give me a hand with that stretcher. The man's skull is fractured. I've got to get him to an operating room as fast as possible!"

The ambulance driver acquiesced readily, and Wentworth took one end of the stretcher, the driver the other. They marched out on the floor, carrying the unconscious vice-president of the store. Wentworth had covered Tynan's head and face with gauze which he had taken from the intern's bag, and no one recognized Tynan. Neither did any one think of looking into the face of the intern carrying the stretcher for the features of Richard Wentworth, whom they were hunting all over the building.

Wentworth's immediate worry was that he should not meet the driver of the Mercy Hospital ambulance; for the driver would at once spot him as a fraud. His eyes darted about constantly, on guard for such a contingency. But they reached the Fifth Avenue entrance unchallenged. Here, a police sergeant was in charge of the doorway, and they were shooing away the crowd that tried to push out.

Wentworth's heart chilled. He knew that sergeant—Hickens by name—and Hickens knew him. It was impossible that he should be able to pass through that doorway, carrying the rear end of the stretcher, without the sergeant's recognizing him. THE DRIVER, at the front end of the stretcher, was already saying to the sergeant: "Fractured skull, Sarge. Emergency. The doc back here wants to rush him to the operating table."

Hickens nodded, glanced first down at the bandage-swathed head of the limp Tynan. Then he started to raise his eyes toward the Spider. Wentworth tensed. His eyes darkened. Was this to be the end? Was he to be cornered here just as he was winning his way out? He would make a try for it, anyway. The police guns might cut him down, but he'd chance it. His body was taut as Hickens' eyes rose.

And just then a woman's shrill voice cut through the assorted noises in the store—a voice that Wentworth recognized with a chill, the voice of Issoris! *"That's Wentworth! Stop him! Stop Wentworth!"*

The Spider glanced over his shoulder, saw the Princess Issoris leaning over the rail, a small pistol in her hand, and pointing directly at himself. She was still shrieking her exhortation to capture Wentworth. They were separated by almost half the width of the huge floor, and Hickens looked wildly about for the person she was pointing at, never thinking that it could be the white-coated intern who held the stretcher, not two feet away from him.

96

Hickens' glance had completely passed over Wentworth at the sound of Issoris' voice. She had defeated her own purpose by shouting her warning at just that instant, for in another moment Wentworth would have been exposed. She had saved him instead of betraying him!

While Hickens glanced feverishly in every direction, Wentworth pushed the stretcher ahead, urging the driver to move on. The driver passed through the doorway, and Wentworth came after him, both hands occupied with holding the stretcher, and not daring to hurry too much.

Behind, Issoris was frantically shouting: "That's Wentworth! That intern is Wentworth! Stop him, you fools!" But in her eagerness to capture the Spider, she made a mistake.

She was leaning over the rail as she shouted, and seeing her quarry about to pass through the doorway to safety, she raised her gun and fired, just as she was shouting. The barking report of her gun drowned her own words! The slug missed Wentworth by a matter of inches, and buried itself in the floor. Hickens jumped, shouted: "Quit that, damn you!"

Issoris screamed another warning, but her shot had startled the frayed nerves of the crowd, and the resultant shouting prevented Hickens from hearing her.

In the meantime, the Spider was already outside. The driver looked back, said: "We'll find the Mercy Hospital ambulance—"

"Never mind," Wentworth said hastily. "Quick! Put him in the nearest ambulance! There's no time!"

They loaded the unconscious Tynan into the first ambulance

at the curb. The driver said doubtfully: "I don't know where the driver of this bus is. Wait! I find him—"

"Don't bother," the Spider snapped. "I'll take him in myself, and bring the ambulance back right away."

The driver shrugged, watched while Wentworth scrambled up behind the wheel. As the motor turned over, Hickens and several uniformed cops came tearing out of the store. They had finally gotten the gist of what Issoris was trying to tell them. Hickens yelled: "Hey! Stop or I'll shoot!"

CHAPTER 7
UNDERGROUND FLIGHT

FIFTH AVENUE was a scene of wild confusion. On the sidewalk there still lay the body of Lawrence Fremont, as well as the bodies of the leper men whom Wentworth and the police had shot. Crowds thronged the sidewalks, held back by police, and motor traffic had been detoured to make room for ambulances and squad cars.

A dozen guns were turned toward Wentworth's ambulance as Hickens called his command to halt. Wentworth paid no attention to the sergeant's order. He threw the gear into low gear, swung the wheel hard away from the curb, and the ambulance leaped ahead.

Hickens cursed, and fired once, twice, then emptied his gun. The windshield in front of Wentworth's face was shattered into a thousand pieces, but luckily the shots came from behind, and the flying fragments of the glass spread to either side instead of smashing into his eyes. Other guns joined the blasting attack on the fleeing ambulance, and the Spider felt the machine shiver under the fusillade. But they were all shooting high, for fear of hitting the milling throng in the street.

Two policemen ran out into the gutter, brandishing their guns, directly in the path of the ambulance. The Spider's lips tightened, and he held the wheel steady, driving straight at them. The policemen fired once each, then leaped aside as the ambulance bore down on them. Wentworth drove through the attacking police like a mad juggernaut, scattering all opposition. More slugs tore through the body from behind, and he feared that Tynan might be hit.

But he dared not stop. Police radio cars were pulling away from the curb in pursuit, and he could hear the swift chugging of a motorcycle catching up to him. The afternoon dusk had deepened into night, and he switched on his headlights, made a sharp right turn on Fifty-Seventh Street, then raced eastward. Peering back through the grilled opening behind him, he could see two police cars close at his heels, careening around the corner. A bluecoat on the running board of the leading car was clinging to the door and firing at the ambulance tires. The motorcycle at his left had pulled up alongside by now, and the cop who was riding it raised a gun to snap a shot at Wentworth. AND AT that moment, the cop on the running board of the pursuing squad car scored a hit on the right rear tire. The tire went with a spiteful explosion, and the ambulance slewed sickeningly toward the motorcycle, with Wentworth fighting the wheel desperately, but not letting up on the gas for one instant.

The motorcycle cop dropped his gun, and frantically twisted his handlebars to the left to avoid the slewing ambulance. Wentworth succeeded in straightening out the machine by a superb bit of driving, but the motorcycle struck the curb, and the cop was thrown from it onto the sidewalk.

Wentworth got just a glimpse of the cop picking himself up, and then faced quickly forward, driving with desperate singleness of purpose, giving her all the gas she would take in spite of the flat tire. The quick, slapping, repetitious sounds of the flat warned him that he couldn't go far before the wheel would smash under the un-cushioned impacts with the ground. But he kept on, past Madison, past Park Avenue, and swung right into Lexington, with his ambulance bell going full blast.

Cars swung out of his path at the urgent signal, and traffic cops cleared the way for him. Behind him, the squad cars were losing out, because traffic has a natural tendency to close in after the passage of an ambulance, and it took extra moments before they could cut through. The police had stopped shooting now, for there was real danger of hitting pedestrians or occupants of other cars.

NITA VAN SLOAN

At Forty-Second Street, the right rear wheel of the ambulance gave under the terrific pounding to which it was being subjected. It cracked, buckled, and the ambulance tipped dangerously as it dragged the end of its axle along the asphalt.

Wentworth fought the wheel like a demon, kept the machine from tipping over, and brought it to a stop in the middle of the street. The police cars were almost a block behind, fighting their way through the late traffic. Wentworth leaped from the driver's seat, while a throng watched in lively curiosity from the curb.

He ran around to the rear, dragged open the door, and jumped inside.

Tynan was sitting up dazedly, with a hand to his head. He looked at Wentworth dully, asked: "Where—what—"

That was all he got a chance to say. Wentworth crashed a fist to his jaw for the second time, and he passed out. The Spider dragged him out, heaved him to his shoulder again. The first of the squad cars was racing toward him past the Forty-Second Street intersection as Wentworth ran with his burden to the curb, and slipped through the subway entrance which was part of the tall building before which he had stopped.

There were mad shouts behind him as he raced down the steps, clinging to his burden with one hand, and to the railing with the other. A uniformed figure loomed at the head of the stairs above him, and a shot whined down past him, to ricochet from the tiled floor beneath. Another followed it, barely missing him. The sounds of the heavy service revolver's explosions were partially drowned by the roar of an incoming express train on the level below.

Wentworth turned a corner, ran with the unconscious Tynan, descended a second set of steps, and raced through the open gate alongside the row of turnstiles giving entrance to the platform. A guard at this gate attempted to stop him but jumped aside as the pursuing cop fired, the shot clattering into the iron gate.

Wentworth was breathing hard from the exertion of carrying Tynan's dead weight. But he did not pause, calling on the reserves of additional energy which his superbly trained body was capable of furnishing to carry him at a fast run toward the subway train alongside the platform. This was the train that he had heard pulling in, and its doors were just beginning to slide shut to the accompaniment of the station master's bell which was clanging now at the rear end of the platform.

NEW YORK subway trains are equipped with automatic safety devices which prevent the doors from closing on a person entering, and injuring him. As Wentworth pushed through the narrowing opening of the car, he touched the rubber bumper along the edge of the door, and it automatically slid back once more.

The train platform was crowded with home-going workers, and Wentworth had to shove to make room for himself and his burden. The door started to slide closed once more, and the nearest of the pursuing policemen lunged forward, threw himself into the car, piling on to Wentworth. He had not dared to shoot again into the press of commuters. Now, however, he grunted: "Got you!" and raised his clubbed revolver to smash down upon the Spider's head.

Women in the packed car screamed, and the crowd pressed away from the two combatants. The door slid shut behind the cop, and the train got into motion. At the same time the cop's revolver came down in a smashing blow at Wentworth's head. Wentworth had no choice but to act as he did. He shifted slightly, with a quick weaving movement of his shoulders, and the blow, aimed at his head, came down upon the shoulder of the unconscious Tynan with crushing force.

The cop cursed, and raised his gun to strike again. Wentworth let go of Tynan and raised both his hands, the bent thumbs

PRINCESS ISSORIS

VARA KUN

seeking twin spots about an inch below the policeman's collar bone. Few men are aware of the fact that strong pressure upon those spots will produce intense pain, and virtual paralysis of the arms. For at these spots are found the muscles known as *pectoralis major* and *pectoralis minor,* which connect the ventral walls of

TANG-AKHMUT

YAHATMA

the chest with the bicipital ridge of the *humerus,* or upper bone of the arm and shoulder. Prolonged pressure upon these muscles may even cause death by hemorrhage.*

It was upon these two spots that Wentworth's thumbs bored with merciless pressure, forcing the cop's shoulders back against the door. The policeman squirmed, twisted in a vain effort to escape that deadly pressure, but Wentworth's strength held him

---

* AUTHOR'S NOTE: It is a well known fact among adventurers and men who live perilous lives in devious places that there is a method of hand-to-hand fighting much mare deadly than the average rough-and-tumble-with-no-holds-barred, about which we hear so much. This other method of fighting has never been given an official name, except that it is often miscalled jiu-jitsu. It is far different from the ancient Japanese science of using the principles of balance and leverage; for this method of fighting implies a thorough knowledge of human anatomy, of the location of muscles and tendons which will yield to pressure. Adventurers will tell you, in unguarded moments, of lean men in various parts of the world who teach this method of fighting—not for money, but out of friendship only. These teachers consider that their knowledge is a trust, to be administered carefully, and to be imparted only to the worthy; for such knowledge in the hands of the unscrupulous or the conscienceless may result in much misery and suffering if not used for a worthy purpose. It is said that in this man-to-man fighting code, there are 27 "touches" that will disable with great agony, and 9 "touches" that will cause painful death. How Richard Wentworth acquired this lethal knowledge, and what tests he had to undergo to qualify as an initiate, will some day make a story in themselves—if I can ever get permission to relate it.

there. The man's face became green, his eyes rolled in agony, and he opened his mouth to cry out. His arms hung powerless at his sides, and the revolver dropped to the floor from suddenly nerveless fingers.

As soon as the policeman released his grip on the revolver, Wentworth eased up the pressure of his thumbs, bent at the knees and came up with the whole weight of his body behind the bunched fist that caught the cop under the chin. The officer was literally lifted from his feet by the smashing blow. WENTWORTH ALLOWED him to sag to the floor, then twisted around to see that the close-pressed crowd around him were watching with wide eyes. No one dared to interfere. New Yorkers had had terrible evidence in the past few months of the folly of intervening or meddling in any way in a fracas in the streets or public places of the city.

For the virtual reign of terror which Tang-akhmut had introduced had made life cheap in New York. For months, Tang-akhmut's servants had fought openly in the streets with police and with Wentworth's allies. Citizens had been shot down, knifed and strangled.

It was true that there had been little activity of such nature during the past month, since Tang-akhmut's disappearance. But other disorders occurred daily. The police force, which had been devitalized and weakened by the intrigues of the so-called Living Pharaoh, was still badly disorganized. Hundreds of patrolmen who had been in the pay or in the power of Tang-akhmut had been necessarily dismissed. With their Commissioner, Kirkpatrick, in jail on a trumped-up murder charge, the

107

remaining police worked with greatly weakened morale, not knowing from whom to take orders.

And in the last few days the mysterious crimes which were rumored to be occurring all over town had made people even more jittery. When a citizen saw men brawling with or without weapons, he gave them a wide berth, just as the subway passengers did now. Beyond crowding away as far as they could from the combatants, they tried to act as if nothing were happening.

This aided Wentworth considerably. He bent quickly, and pocketed the policeman's fallen gun, just as the train rumbled into the Fourteenth Street Station.

The Spider lifted the still unconscious Tynan to his shoulder again, and when the door slid open he stepped quickly out on the platform. His anxious gaze scanned the crowded station for signs of bluecoats. He knew that it was just possible for his pursuers at Forty-Second Street to have called headquarters and for headquarters to have radioed prowl cars in the neighborhood to watch all stations south of Forty-Second. Still, the running time of the express train from Forty-Second to Fourteenth was only six minutes, and there might still be a small margin of safety for him.

Though many people threw curious glances at the white-coated, muscular hospital intern who carried the unconscious form of a man over his shoulder like a sack of flour, no one offered to stop him as he mounted the steps of the kiosk, and came out into Union Square. He breathed deeply of the fresh night air, but did not put his burden down.

Union Square recalled painful memories to him. It was only

a block from here that the final clash with Tang-akhmut had taken place, less than a month ago. Down the street was the tall building which had housed the Finney Finance Company, the financial headquarters of Tang-akhmut. It was the Spider's raid upon those headquarters, aided by a band of Chinese gunrunners, which had broken the power of the Living Pharaoh. But Tang-akhmut himself had escaped. That was a bitter pill for Wentworth to swallow, especially in view of the events that had taken place today.

But he wasted little time in retrospection. People were staring at him, though the traffic cop at the busy intersection had not yet seen him. He stepped to the curb with his burden, and pulled open the door of a cab parked at the curb, close to the subway entrance.

"Drive to Chinatown!" he snapped.

THE CABBY threw a backward glance at his white coat, saw the *"Mercy Hospital"* inscribed on his sleeve, and said: "What's the idea, doc? Your joint is uptown—"

"I know all that," Wentworth barked "Suppose you drive, and never mind the questions. There's ten dollars in it for you."

The driver grinned. "That's different, doc. For ten bucks I'm the Sphinx!" He pulled the car away, caught the green light at the corner, and sped down Fourth Avenue.

Wentworth was going to the only place in the city where he was sure he would be free of molestation by the police—or by the agents of Tang-akhmut. That was the prearranged meeting place of which Nita van Sloan had spoken—the place to which Ram Singh was bringing the cripple, Chenab Sind. There in Chinatown, among his Oriental friends, Richard Wentworth would have the leisure to question Tynan, to take stock of the situation, and to try to ferret out the motive behind the wanton raid of the Leper Men upon the great department store of Fremont and Tynan.

While Wentworth's cab carried him swiftly southward to Chinatown, another sedan was bearing Ram Singh and Chenab Sind in the same direction. But Wentworth could not know that Ram Singh's car was being followed; nor could he know that he had just missed seeing Nita, back there at Fremont and Tynan's. Neither was there any means by which he could know that certain other eyes, eyes of a person less harried by the police at that moment, had spotted Nita van Sloan in front of the Fifth Avenue department store at the very moment when he had missed seeing her.

Had Richard Wentworth possessed all that information as he sped southward toward Chinatown that evening, then much of the trend of subsequent events might have been changed.

WHEN WENTWORTH'S cab reached Chinatown, he tapped on the window and said to the driver: "Turn into Doyers Street, and park halfway down the block under that street lamp."

The cabby shrugged, and obeyed instructions. Wentworth had propped Tynan up in the seat beside him, and the department store executive was breathing deeply and regularly.

The Spider moved over toward the window near the curb, and sat so that the light from the street lamp shone full upon his face. Shuffling yellow men were passing, with here and there a white person. There were dozens of cars parked at the curb, and no one glanced in through the window.

The building before which they were parked was a three-story, faded brick structure. On the ground floor was a single store that occupied its entire width. There were Chinese characters in one corner of the plate glass window, while across the upper part appeared the wording:

NORTH CHINA CURIO COMPANY
Importers of Antiques and Objects of Interest

The cab driver turned his head, asked: "How long we got to stay here, mister?"

"Just have patience, my friend," Wentworth told him.

They waited another few minutes, while Wentworth kept his face in the light. At last, the door of the North China Curio Company opened, and a tall, powerful, rawboned Chinaman emerged. He looked up and down the street carefully, then crossed over to the taxi.

His eyes flickered in recognition, and he spoke in Cantonese: "Yang Chung bids you welcome, illustrious visitor. It is safe for you to enter—"

Wentworth interrupted, also speaking in Cantonese, with the ease of one who has lived long among the Chinese: "I knew your lookout would see me, Lee. Tell Yang Chung that I have an unconscious man with me, and I do not wish to be seen carrying him in. Neither do I want the driver of this car to know where I go. Can he arrange it?"

Lee nodded. "Without a doubt. I go to arrange it at once."

111

He bowed jerkily, made his way back into the store.

The cabby had been listening to the conversation. "Geez, doc, you can sure sling that lingo. What do we do now?"

"Take it easy, friend. We'll be through soon."

The Spider no longer kept his face in the light. Now that he had accomplished his purpose, he sat back, and gave his attention to Tynan. The man was stirring, feebly regaining consciousness. Wentworth hoped he would stay under for another short while.

After what seemed an age of waiting, a long black sedan pulled up alongside the cab. A Chinese chauffeur was at the wheel, and Lee and another yellow man were within. Wentworth sighed relievedly, and pushed open the taxi door on the side of the sedan. Lee and his companion got out of the sedan, and without being told they helped Wentworth to transfer Tynan's body into their car.

Then Wentworth gave the cabby two ten-dollars bills. "One is for doing as you were told. The other is for keeping mum about this. Get it?"

The driver nodded eagerly. "I get you, doc. I've forgot about it already!"

The cab drove off, and after a moment the sedan with Wentworth, Tynan and the Chinamen started down the block, turned a corner and made another sharp turn into an alley. The alley ran down for perhaps twenty feet to the double doors of a garage which opened as the sedan approached, and they rolled into it. The doors closed behind them.

Neither Wentworth nor Lee noticed the Hindu in the small

coupé, who had followed Ram Singh from Nita's apartment. That coupé was parked near the corner, and as soon as the Chinamen's sedan had pulled into the alley, the Hindu slid out of his coupé, hurried to the corner and entered a drug store, sidled into a telephone booth.

HE DIALED a number, then spoke in Hindustani. "I have great success, master," he reported. "I followed the Sikh with Chenab Sind to the house of the Chinaman, Yang Chung. It is over the store of the North China Curio Company. And just now, master, I saw another come. Wentworth himself. Master, Wentworth is within that house!"

An approving voice came from the other end. "You have done well, Laska. You have the leper with you in the car?"

"Yes, master. He waits in the car. He is anxious to die."

"Good. Let him go out and die, as he has been instructed. Wait there and watch what happens. And phone again."

"Yes, master."

The Hindu went back to the car. Now it could be noticed that there was another person in there besides him. In the darkness the black rubber hood was hardly noticeable. The Hindu exchanged a few words with the leper, the hooded man nodded, stepped out of the car, and ran toward the alley where the garage was located.

Inside the garage, two of the big Chinamen carried Tynan up two flights of stairs, while Lee and Wentworth followed. In a sumptuous room furnished in the oriental manner, Yang Chung greeted Wentworth. These two had fought together against Tang-akhmut, and Yang Chung had benefited greatly thereby.

Now he was the Spider's staunchest ally. He spoke in Cantonese, which Wentworth understood as well as he did English.

"There are two who await you in the next room, Wentworth *san*. They are your servant, Ram Singh, and a strange, legless man, who has but one arm. They arrived but a moment ago."

Wentworth started, and frowned. He had ordered Ram Singh to stay with Nita. What had happened? But just then the old, gray-bearded Chinese doctor whom Yang Chung kept on his payroll stood up from beside the cot where they had placed the unconscious form of Tynan. He spoke in singsong Cantonese to Yang Chung, but looked at Wentworth. "This man whom you have brought—you wished to have him talk?"

Wentworth nodded. "Yes. There are some things that he knows—"

The old doctor shook his head. "He will never talk again, this miserable physician informs you. The man is dead!"

"Dead! Why, he was alive not fifteen minutes ago. I had to knock him out—"

"True, but he is dead. I should say that he died of heart failure. He must have sustained a severe shock recently. His heart gave out."

"Thank you," Wentworth said bitterly. He had gone to the risk of carrying Tynan all that distance, exposing himself to police bullets, only to have him die in this way. Whatever he knew was locked within his stiffening lips. Wentworth was back where he had started so far as his knowledge of Tang-akhmut's operations was concerned.

He watched wearily while the doctor covered the dead Tynan

REIGN OF THE SNAKE MEN

with a bright yellow robe which he picked up from a chair. Then, when the doctor was gone, Wentworth said to Yang Chung: "I might as well see Ram Singh and the one with him. I suppose it's more bad news."

Yang Chung clapped his hands twice, and in a moment Ram Singh and Chenab Sind were led in. Wentworth said sternly: "Ram Singh! I ordered you to remain with Nita!"

"*Wah*, master," the Sikh exclaimed disgustedly. "She has a mind of her own, the *memsahib*." He related how Chenab Sind had appeared and how he had repulsed the attack of the Hindus under the snake-master; and how Nita had decided to go to Fremont and Tynan's.

"So," he ended, "I brought this misbegotten spawn of the devil to speak with thee, master. But I do not trust him!"

Chenab Sind had remained silent all this time, eyeing Wentworth and Yang Chung. Now as Wentworth looked at him questioningly, feeling a twinge of pity for the cripple, Chenab Sind said: "I will not waste time trying to convince you of my good faith. Your man saw me attacked at Miss van Sloan's house. Now I will tell you what I came for. *I can show you where Tang-akhmut hides!*"

WENTWORTH'S EYES narrowed. "Who are you? How do you know where Tang-akhmut is hiding?"

"Who I am is not important. My name you already know, and it means nothing to you. But in India I was known as a great physician, and a chemist. That was before I became—as I am." He glanced down at the stumps of his legs. "I seek vengeance on the man who made me this way—Tang-akhmut. I ask only that you take me with you, so that I can witness the end of the Living Pharaoh!"

Wentworth made a sudden decision. "All right, I'll trust you. But you haven't told me yet—"

"Where to find the Man from the East? I will tell you now." He moved nearer on his stumps. His voice dropped, and came in a queer whisper from that great, ungainly head. "Tang-akhmut has chosen a hiding place that could never be discovered. There he has gathered desperate men whom he rescued from the penal colony in Guiana; also, he brought a hundred lepers from the leper settlement. He brought them in a ship that he chartered in Brazil. He landed them at night, and transported them by twos and threes to this hiding place of his, which he has made into an impregnable fortress."

Wentworth broke in impatiently. "Well, man, name it. Where's this impregnable headquarters?"

Chenab Sind licked his lips. "You know the transverse automobile road that goes through your Central Park at Seventy-Ninth Street from Central Park West to Fifth Avenue?"

"Yes, yes, of course."

"Well, there is a police station there, no? That station was abandoned some time ago, because your W.P.A. workers were widening the tunnel. But the project was abandoned because they found they would have to blast. However, the station house has never been used again, for the precinct was joined to another one. It is in that abandoned station house that Tang-akhmut has his headquarters! Was it not a stroke of genius?"

116

Yang Chung exclaimed: "Good! I will summon my hatchet men, and we will raid him—"

Chenab Sind shook his head. "You would all die. Tang-akhmut has powerful gasses which he could release against you. Not a man would reach the inside of that station house. And if you did, you would not live for five minutes."

Wentworth asked softly: "What do you suggest?"

Chenab Sind shrugged. "That is for you to decide. I have done my part."

At that moment Lee entered. He spoke excitedly in Cantonese to Yang Chung. "A strange thing has happened. A hooded man, a leper, was skulking outside the garage. Sam Foo caught him, and the man struggled. Sam Foo had to kill him. He must have followed Wentworth *san* here from uptown. It is strange that he should have come here—"

Chenab Sind's eyes sparkled. "If it is one of Tang-akhmut's lepers, there is your chance to get into his headquarters, Richard Wentworth—if you are brave enough. Paint the symbol of the cobra upon your chest, don the hood, and lo, you have the perfect disguise!"

The Spider regarded the cripple thoughtfully.

THE MAN might be sincere in his avowed hatred of Tang-akhmut. On the other hand, this might all be an elaborate trap. But he had walked into traps deliberately before. "You think I could get in?"

Chenab Sind nodded. "I'm sure you could. I'll go with you."

"I thought that Tank-akhmut's—men were after you."

"They were," the cripple's lips twisted. "But they will hesitate

117

As the knife men rushed, Wentworth raised Chenab Sind

from the floor and hurled him straight at Yahatma.

before killing me. You see, I am the only one who knows the formula for the drug that is a sure antidote for leprosy. They need my medical knowledge, and my skill in chemistry. They sought merely to prevent my visiting Miss van Sloan. But if I return, they will welcome me. Once inside, I can provide you with arms. The rest will be up to you."

"Why can't I bring my own weapons?"

"Because no one is permitted to enter that place with weapons. You saw those lepers chaise against the police unarmed. If a gun were found on you, it would arouse suspicion at once."

Wentworth glanced at Yang Chung, who shrugged. "I like it not, Wentworth *san*. Is it necessary that you thrust yourself alone into danger? Perhaps you could notify the police—"

Chenab Sind laughed shrilly. "The police! One burst of gas would dispose of them. I know. I developed that gas myself!"

Wentworth suddenly made his decision. "I'll go! But remember, Chenab Sind, I'll be watching you sharply. The first false move you make—"

"Will be my last!" the cripple finished for him sardonically. "You will never know until the end, Wentworth, whether I am to be trusted or not! Yet—" he added thoughtfully, "you are a very brave man. There is a chance that you may beat Tang-akhmut!"

Wentworth swung on Yang Chung. "Have that leper brought up. I'll have to wear his hood, but I guess there won't be much danger, since I haven't any scratches on my face."

"Find some paint—red paint," Chenab Sind ordered. "I have only one hand, but I can paint a good duplicate of the cobra on your chest. Strip to the waist, Wentworth. You are about to become a leper man!"

CHAPTER 8
AT PHARAOH'S THRONE

NITA VAN SLOAN had driven directly to Fremont and Tynan's from her apartment on Central Park West. Had she left *after* Ram Singh instead of before, she might have seen the car that trailed him. As it was, she knew nothing of it. By that small decision she had unconsciously set in motion a train of monstrous events that would rebound against both herself as well as the man she loved.

Now, however, her one thought, her one anxiety, was to discover as quickly as possible what was happening at Fremont and Tynan's. Every fiber of her being told her that Richard Wentworth had walked into some sort of trap at the department store. As yet she had no inkling of the dreadful raid that had taken place there.

So then when she turned the corner into Fifth Avenue in her small coupé, the vista of slaughter and tumult that opened up before her sent a creeping terror up her spine. There was a police line here which prevented cars from entering the block, but Nita could see the twisted body of Lawrence Fremont, though she did not recognize him from that distance.

She could also see the bodies of the leper men, littering the sidewalk, lying where they had been shot by Strove and Wentworth. She *did* recognize the figure of the coiled cobra carved

121

on the chests of the dead leper men, and she remembered that the flute player, Vara Kun, as well as the men who had attacked Chenab Sind, all wore the same dreadful mark.

All this bore out the things that Chenab Sind had told her. She realized that a plot of unusual magnitude was afoot, a plot that must be fostered by a tremendously clever criminal mentality. As yet she could not find a motive for such hideous doings.

But she thrust all that from her. She must learn where Richard Wentworth was, what he was doing, whether he was alive yet. Her eyes darted about for some one whom she could question, but in her haste she did not see the man with the scar across his left eye, who was watching her from the back of the limousine just around the corner behind her. This was the man who had shot Pierre Robillard; it was the same man whom Wentworth had found at the microphone in the control room. He had fled from Wentworth, and had been able to make his way out of the store, for the cordon of police had not yet been established. He had retreated to the limousine, which had obviously been awaiting him, chauffeured by a dark-skinned Oriental who sat in stolid immobility.

Now, the man with the scar started perceptibly as his single eye spotted Nita van Sloan driving around the corner. He watched avidly while she parked. He rubbed his moist hands together slowly in oily satisfaction, and nodded.

"It is she!" he murmured. "Fortune is good to us!"

The chauffeur turned at the sound of his voice. "Did you speak, Yahatma?" the Oriental asked deferentially, in Hindustani.

"Yes, yes, but to myself. I am going to speak to that young woman in the car. Keep a sharp watch. If I should need you, I will call!"

The chauffeur raised palm to forehead, and bowed his head. "I hear and I obey, Yahatma!"

The man addressed as Yahatma got out of his car and walked quickly to Nita's coupé. Just as she was about to get out herself, he opened the door of her car, and bowed, smiling out of thin lips. His pure white hair, rising in a straight pompadour, failed to soften the malignant lines of his countenance.

"We are well met, Miss van Sloan!"

NITA EYED him with a strange feeling of revulsion. It was not so much the scar and the empty eye socket; it was something subtle, incapable of analysis, which she read in the murky depths of that other eye of his—something that told her this man was the master of strange, evil powers which she could not hope to combat.

"Who are you?" she demanded.

"Those who either love or fear me," he told her with a queer quirk of his thin lips, "call me *Yahatma.*"

Nita resisted the impulse to draw away from him. She forced into her voice a tone of scorn she did not feel. "And those who neither fear nor love you?"

He slipped into the seat beside her. "Dear lady," he said softly, "there are no such—alive!"

Whatever Nita might have answered to that strange statement, she was spared the necessity of saying. For it was at that moment that Richard Wentworth made his exit from the

Fremont and Tynan store, at the rear end of the stretcher which bore the form of John T. Tynan.

She heard the shot that the Princess Issoris fired within the store, and turned her head sharply. All thought of the sinister man beside her fled from her mind as she recognized Richard Wentworth in the white coat of the hospital intern.

She dared not call out to him, for she understood at once that some urgent compulsion had caused him to pose as the ambulance doctor. She watched tensely as Wentworth loaded the still form of Tynan into the rear, and as he vaulted up to the driver's seat. She saw Sergeant Hickens come running out, saw Wentworth start the ambulance away from the curb with the police close after him, and firing as they came.

She cried out: "Dick! Dick!" without any expectation of his hearing her. Her motor was running and she saw at once how she could help him. She could swing her car in behind the fleeing ambulance and block the pursuit; it would give Wentworth a chance to put distance between himself and the squad cars—even if it did mean her own capture. That did not worry her; as long as Wentworth made good his escape.

All thought of the man who called himself Yahatma was forgotten as her hand flew to the gear shift lever and her foot sought the accelerator. But she touched neither. For at that precise instant, the one-eyed Yahatma raised his open palm behind her head, and brought the edge of his hand down in a sharp blow at the base of her skull.

The blow sent her forward in her seat, driving the blood from her brain, numbing all her faculties, though she did not lose consciousness. She heard Yahatma murmur: "A brave woman indeed! We shall see how brave you can really be!"

She wanted to open her mouth, to scream, to beat him away from her with her fists. But her body refused to obey the impulses from her brain. It would be many minutes before she could once more direct the muscles of her body. And while she slumped thus helpless, while the ambulance driven by Wentworth careened around the corner with the police in mad pursuit, she felt herself moved along the seat, felt Yahatma's cold, almost reptilian breath on her neck as he slipped past her and slid under the wheel.

She was conscious of motion, of the coupé purring smoothly away from the curb. In a moment they had made a complete turn, and were heading away from Fifth Avenue in a direction opposite to the one taken by Wentworth's ambulance.

NITA FELT the blood coming back into her arteries, felt a resurgence of strength, and endeavored to sit up. The spot at the base of her skull, where she had been struck, was still sore, and the whole back of her head ached. There was a blur before her eyes, and she clutched wildly at the wheel. Suddenly the coupé came to an abrupt stop as Yahatma braked it hard.

In an instant, the chauffeur of the sedan, which had followed them, came to the door, carrying a length of silken twine. Yahatma took the twine, twisted Nita's hands cruelly, and wound the twine around her wrists so tight that she felt her fingers growing numb.

Yahatma was chuckling. He took a heavy strip of turban cloth which the chauffeur now gave him, and wrapped it around Nita's head, covering her eyes.

"This," he explained, "is to prevent you from seeing where you are to be taken. Your friend, Wentworth, my dear young lady, is a very clever and a very daring young man. I foresee that we shall have much difficulty with him—if we do not plan something drastic for him. Perhaps my meeting with you was very fortunate. No?"

Nita made no answer, though she could have spoken without trouble through the folds of the turban cloth. She allowed Yahatma's bony hands to push her down on to the floor of the coupé. He said: "It will be best to make no resistance, Miss van Sloan—if you do not wish to be knocked on the head."

She knew that he would do just that, so she lay quietly on the floorboard while Yahatma drove swiftly. She tried to orient herself, to follow his turns so as to get an idea of the direction they were taking.

She noted that he drove west, in the direction in which he had started, for what might have been a block; that would make it Sixth Avenue. He stopped for a traffic light there, then drove on, slowed at what seemed to be a corner, then passed it. Seventh Avenue, then Central Park West. Nita couldn't be sure of her distances, but she judged it was at Central Park West that he made a wide curve and turned north. That would be around the edge of the park. If her calculations were right, he was now driving up Central Park West, where she lived. She tried to imagine the streets as they drove up—Fifty-ninth, Sixtieth, Sixty-first....

The dizziness in her head, from that blow, caused her to lose count. Now she didn't know how far up they had gone. She felt the car slow up, come to a stop, but she heard the gears being shifted back into first. That meant he was waiting for a traffic light to change. Probably Seventy-Second, probably Eighty-First, or maybe Eighty-Sixth. She knew there were traffic cops at those three corners, though recently, since the demoralization of the police force, traffic direction had been cut to a minimum.

As the motor throbbed while they waited for the change of light, Nita heard the traffic officer's whistle at the corner. One blast was the signal for the cross traffic to stop. Immediately after it came a second blast, at which north-and-south traffic would move.

The car got in motion, and Nita's throbbing brain worked quickly. Ten feet from the white line to the center of the intersection where the cop would be standing... They should be abreast of him now.

Abruptly Nita raised her head, shouted at the top of her lungs through the cloth that enveloped her head: *"Help! Kidnapers!"*

She repeated the words again and again, and her voice rose loud over the sound of the motor. She felt the engine throbbing as Yahatma fed it more and more gas. The car spurted ahead, and she could distinctly hear behind them the stentorian roar of the traffic officer: *"Hey you! Stop that car!"*

BUT THEIR speed increased instead of diminishing, and in a moment Nita felt the coupé shudder as a high-powered thirty-eight caliber slug from a police positive smashed into the rear framework of the tonneau. On the floor where she lay, it seemed to her that the coupé was roaring along at eighty miles an hour.

127

Another shot crashed the rear window, and bits of glass tinkled about her head. Still Yahatma did not stop, but kept the coupé headed straight north.

Two more shots smashed into the car, and then suddenly the firing ceased. It was as if the cop had given up the battle.

Then, Nita heard Yahatma's wicked chuckle from directly above her. "That was very brave of you, young lady. Perhaps you are surprised that the police officer does not pursue us with further shots? Shall I tell you why? It is because my faithful servant, Abdul, was following us in my sedan. Abdul ran down your brave policeman. The worthy officer will soon be on his way either to the hospital or the morgue!"

Nita shuddered at the callous way in which this man told her of another man's death. She wondered what sort of monster he was, what was his purpose in abducting her, what was back of the ghastly raid at Fremont and Tynan's as well as of the attempt that had been made upon her in her own apartment.

Yahatma was saying: "We are almost at our destination, young lady, and there will be no more traffic officers; otherwise, I should have to knock you on the head again. You are entirely too talky!"

She did not answer, and after a few moments of silent driving, she felt the car swinging in another right turn. She couldn't tell now where they were. She had lost all sense of direction.

While she was wondering, the car came to a stop.

Yahatma lifted her up by the arms, guided her out of the car, and up two short steps. Then he led her, gripping her arm tightly, through two doorways.

At last he guided her into a room, shut the door behind them, and said: "You see, Vara Kun, where you failed, I have succeeded. Behold, the young lady whom you attempted to capture your-self—Miss van Sloan!"

AS HE spoke he yanked the turban cloth from off her head, and Nita blinked her eyes, looked at the queer, white-vested figure of the glittering eyed snake-charmer whom she had last seen from her apartment window.

"You—you eliminated Wentworth?" Vara Kun asked eagerly.

"Alas, no. He escaped in an ambulance, very cleverly. He almost caught me in the control room of the store. That man is a dangerous enemy. I trust that the presence of Miss van Sloan here may help to blunt the edge of his danger to us."

Nita said proudly: "You are mistaken, Yahatma. Richard Wentworth will never permit anything to stand in the way of his war with Tang-akhmut. I would have little respect for him if he did!"

Yahatma nodded, and seized her by the arm, forced her across the room, with Vara Kun following closely. Nita did not attempt to struggle, for she recognized the strength that lay behind the bony fingers of that grip. They passed through a second room, whose walls were as bare as those of the first.

They entered a third room, and Nita started in sudden revulsion.

THIS CHAMBER was much larger than the first two, and it was literally crowded with black-hooded, bare-chested men, bearing the symbol of the circle and the coiled cobra.

Yahatma spoke to them in a smooth, calm voice: "You may

rest, my children. Soon the master shall send you forth to die, so that you may be reborn again in well bodies. Have patience!"

She was glad when they passed through this room, into a corridor. This corridor had cold stone floors, and on either side was a row of cells, with iron grilled doors.

Yahatma swung open one of these doors, and pushed Nita into it. He laughed harshly. "Soon the Living Pharaoh will see you. In the meantime—" his voice assumed an edge of sardonic humor—"try to make yourself comfortable."

There was only a single light which burned dully in the corridor outside the row of cells, and by its light Nita found a bare cot upon which she sat. Her brows furrowed in thought as she tried to think of where this strange place could be located.

She was startled out of her train of thought by a small voice that seemed to come almost from beside her: *"Hello, lady! Are you as scared as I am?"*

NITA TURNED swiftly. There was nobody in the cell with her. Where had that little voice come from? She glanced about, and suddenly a wry smile tugged at her lips. There, in the cell next to hers, with head close to the separating bars, was a small girl.

The child's lips quivered. She sat up, wiped her eyes with the back of her hand, and suddenly broke into a smile. She snuggled up close to the bars, put her thin hand through and Nita clasped it in both of her own. The girl spoke with a sort of trusting childishness.

"I'm Elaine Robillard. Some men came to our house, and hit my nurse on the head, and took me away. They brought me here. It was that man who only has one eye. I think he's a very bad man."

"Elaine Robillard! Does your family own the jewelry store on Fifth Avenue?"

"That's right. My grandpa Pierre owns it. My father and mother were killed in an accident three years ago. Grandpa takes care of me. Grandpa is awful nice. I think you're nice too. What's your name?"

"Nita van Sloan, my darling."

"Will they hurt us?"

"Of course not. Don't you worry. They won't hurt you. You're too sweet to hurt—even for them!"

Nita's heart went out to little, red-haired Elaine. Just such a child, she imagined, might have been hers and Richard's. Often had she given reign to fancy on a lonely night, dreaming that she and Richard Wentworth were happily married, with all this constant peril forever behind them. Nita hid it well from Wentworth, but the mother instinct was strong within her. All her dreams always included a little one like Elaine. Impulsively she lifted the thin, cold hand through the bars, and kissed it.

Elaine Robillard cried softly. "You're lovely, Nita. When these bad men let us go, you must come to our house and meet Grandpa. I think I'll make Grandpa marry you. Then you can live with us always. Wouldn't that be nice?"

"Wonderful!" Nita breathed. She did not laugh at the childish conceit. Her heart was suddenly torn with pain. She had no illusions about Tang-akhmut or Vara Kun or Yahatma. They would not hesitate to kill this sweet little thing if it served their ends. Now she was thinking of herself not at all, but of Elaine. The child's trusting wistfulness had taken her heart by storm.

At a sound in the corridor, she glanced toward the figure of Yahatma, who had suddenly appeared from the next room. He was followed by two of the half-naked Hindus, with the cobra emblem on their chests. These Hindus seemed to be different from the hooded leper men whom she had encountered on her way in. Although they seemed to be as devoted to their master, and as fanatical—as was evidenced by the one who had leaped from the window of her apartment after failing to kidnap her—they were not afflicted with the dreadful disease. Tang-akhmut had certainly collected a motley crew of miscreants, the ragtag and bobtail of the East.

Wentworth had told her of the interrupted message of Jack Bannister—how he had heard the rumor of the one-eyed man and the snake-doctor and—Bannister's message had stopped there, broken off by the knife of one of these Hindus. But there had also been the cable from the Paris Sûreté, about the French penal settlement and the leper colony. From such a crew there was little for Elaine or herself to hope.

Yahatma opened her door first, and motioned her out, then opened the door of the adjoining cell. Little Elaine shrank back at first, and Nita saw the surge of evil to Yahatma's features, saw him about to step in after the child. So she called out hastily: "Come, Elaine. Come along with me. I guess they want us both!"

Elaine Bannister raised her little chin, and her lips quivered. "I—I'm coming." Slowly she came out of the cell, and rushed over into Nita's arms. Yahatma's teeth showed in a nasty grin, and the livid scar across his face glowed as if it were alive.

"Our master, Tang-akhmut, the Living Pharaoh, will see you both now."

HE STRODE toward the far door, and Nita followed him with Elaine pressed close beside her.

The next room was small, and there was a row of cylindrical tanks along one wall, with peculiar nozzles built at an angle out of their tops.

They followed him through another doorway, and found themselves in a large room, the walls of which were hung with shimmering draperies. This was so different from the bareness of the other rooms that Nita was startled for a moment. Then she understood the reason for the splendor of this chamber. It was the throne room of Tang-akhmut!

There, upon a dais at the far end of the room, sat the bitterest enemy of Richard Wentworth and of the city—the Man from the East, the one who styled himself the Living Pharaoh—Tang-akhmut!

His deep-set eyes were fixed intensely upon Nita and Elaine, as the two advanced slowly toward him, with Yahatma at their side. The one-eyed man bowed low.

"Master, I have succeeded in bringing here the woman you ordered captured. Nita van Sloan. This is she. The child is the granddaughter of Pierre Robillard, who died today for defying us."

At that last statement, Elaine Robillard's eyes opened wide, and a gasp escaped from her childish throat. "Grandpa! Dead! You—you devil! You—killed him!"

She broke from Nita, and began to pound with her little fists against Yahatma's chest, beating against him frantically.

Yahatma stepped back involuntarily before the unexpected onslaught, and Tang-akhmut laughed. Yahatma's face grew red, and his hand stole toward the knife at his girdle.

It flashed in the air above Elaine's head, and he uttered strange, angry oaths in a foreign tongue. The knife was about to descend in a flashing arc, right into the throat of the child, when Nita sprang forward, thrust the child away, and stood under the knife, her breast ready to receive the thrust.

YAHATMA, IN the grip of a tremendous gust of rage, would have plunged that knife into Nita's breast without hesitation but for the sharp lash of Tang-akhmut's voice.

"Yahatma! *Do you too, wish to die?*"

The one-eyed man stiffened as if that voice had been a material weapon and had struck him in the face. Slowly, his face twisting with barely restrained passion, he lowered the knife, and put it back in the sheath at his girdle. He bowed low, murmured: "Forgive me, great lord. I forgot that I was in your presence."

Tang-akhmut motioned with his hand. "You are forgiven. See that you do not forget again!"

He turned to Nita, who had once more clasped Elaine to her bosom.

"Miss van Sloan, the knife is not for you. I have reserved something much more interesting for your—er—amusement— if you refuse to do as I ask. You have seen the tanks of gas in the next room. In the closet there are gas masks. We are fully equipped to destroy a great part of the population of the city of New York if we are balked in our plans. Your friend, Richard Wentworth, is the greatest barrier to our success. The police are fools, and do not worry us."

Nita stood silent, staring at the man who called himself the Living Pharaoh.

Tang-akhmut went on. "It will interest you to know that your friend Wentworth escaped from Fremont and Tynan's in the ambulance. He took Tynan with him, and sought refuge in a certain hiding place that I had not known of before—one that you know of."

Nita started. If Tang-akhmut knew that, then Wentworth was in imminent peril. She listened carefully to the Living Pharaoh.

"He is in the rabbit-warren in Chinatown which is owned by his friend, Yang Chang. Your man, Ram Singh, was followed there, and Wentworth was seen to enter. Now, I wish no further trouble with Wentworth. I propose that you phone him from here, and inform him that you are in my hands. Tell him that you will be inoculated with leprosy unless he promises at once to leave New York, and to interfere no longer with my plans. If he agrees, you will be freed, and allowed to join him. I know I can depend upon his word."

NITA STOOD straight and tall, meeting the gaze of Tang-akhmut. "I would never do it," she said steadily.

His voice grew almost wheedling, as he sought to tempt her. "What do the people of this city mean to you or to Richard Wentworth? I know that he is the Spider. The police of New

135

York hunt him incessantly, the residents look upon him as a pariah. Why not go away, and forget them? No one will think the less of you. And if he persists in fighting me, he will not only lose you, but he will himself be destroyed!"

Nita smiled. "If you are so sure of destroying him, why then do you try to buy him off at the price of my life?"

"Because I must go on with my plans. He is very clever, and very dangerous. I want no interference with my program for the next few days. If all goes well—" he paused, and a certain evil pride shone in his glittering eyes—"I shall have the city within my hands before the week is over!"

Nita shook her head. "My answer is still no. For one thing, Richard Wentworth would be a poor specimen of a man if he allowed my life to stand in the way of ridding the city of you. For another, I could never be happy with him if he accepted peace at the price you demand."

Tang-akhmut did not grow angry. He sighed. "I expected this."

He looked up as the door behind Nita and Elaine opened, and Vara Kun entered. The cobra about the snake-man's neck was writhing as usual as he stepped mincingly across the floor and approached Tang-akhmut. He whispered in the ear of the Living Pharaoh, and Tang-akhmut smiled, nodded.

Vara Kun stepped back, and Tang-akhmut addressed Nita once more.

"You have seen how this cobra strikes. Let me tell you that it is not an ordinary cobra. Its sacs have been emptied of their venom by a difficult operation. In place of the venom there has been inserted a virulent poison known only to us of the East. That poison kills instantly.

"It also has other properties. It will destroy the germs of leprosy if injected within five hours after inoculation. Vara Kun always carries that cobra, both as an offensive weapon, and as a protection for ourselves in case we should be accidentally inoculated.

"Now, suppose I were to promise you and Wentworth enough of this drug to cure all those women who were scratched by my men at Fremont and Tynan's. Would you then agree to leave the city?"

For a moment Nita was tempted. She suspected some sort of trap. She could well believe Tang-akhmut's statement about the cobra, for she had seen how it killed the policeman in front of her apartment. But she knew that the Man from the East would not make such a concession if there were not some catch to it.

Tang-akhmut's eyes rested on Elaine, who had buried her head against Nita's breast.

"Remember too," he said softly, "that the girl would go free with you. You seem to have taken a liking to her."

NITA WAS sorely tempted. After all, it couldn't harm to call Dick. Tang-akhmut knew where he was anyway. The call would warn him that his retreat with Yang Chung had been ferreted out. He could use his own judgment as to what to do. She might even be able to slip in some of the valuable information that she had gleaned from this interview.

She was on the point of agreeing, when the decision was suddenly taken from her by the entrance of the Princess Issoris!

The sister of Tang-akhmut had been standing at the door for a minute or two, watching the scene. Now she burst into the room, her eyes flashing murderous hate at Nita.

"No, no! I won't have it!" Issoris cried. "That woman must die. She must be made to suffer in the vilest way that you know! You promised me!"

The hate which Issoris bore for Nita van Sloan dated back to the day when Wentworth had turned his back on the advances of the sister of the Living Pharaoh.

Now she took a step closer to Nita, moving like an angry, hissing cat. She said through clenched teeth: "When I am through with you, we shall see whether there is anything left that the Spider can love!"

Tang-akhmut frowned. "Sister! This is no time for indulging in spite. Wait until we have supreme power. There will come another time when you can vent your rage against Wentworth and against this woman. I hate him as much as you do—"

Issoris faced him, smiling disdainfully. "Does the Living Pharaoh break a promise? Your word has been given. I demand that you keep it!"

Tang-akhmut hesitated. His proposal to Nita had been dictated by cold judgment, against his own inclination. He longed with every fiber of his evil soul to see Nita writhe under torture, and to see Wentworth forced to watch helplessly. He had made her the proposal of peace only because it would further his own plans. Now he found it easy to accede to his sister's demand, because it pampered his own hate.

"So be it!" he declared. "We will trap Wentworth instead of making peace with him!"

Yahatma took a step toward the dais. "But, master, what of our plans? Must we delay them until we have dealt with Wentworth? Would it not be better to let her phone—"

Tang-akhmut looked at him coldly. "If you disapprove of my methods—"

"No, no!" Yahatma exclaimed hastily. "I bow to the master's will!"

"Then take her and the child back to the cells. As soon as we have dealt with Wentworth, we will amuse our sister with these two." He turned to Issoris. "Does that satisfy you?"

The Princess Issoris smiled slowly, felinely. "It is well, my brother!" she purred. Already her eyes were glowing with the anticipation of the sadistic orgy to come as they roved over the body of Nita van Sloan....

CHAPTER 9
THE MAN IN THE HOOD

NITA WAS thinking of little Elaine. The impact of the monstrous things that were taking place here upon that innocent mind would have an everlasting effect. Silently she allowed herself and the child to be led out of the room by two of the Hindus. Issoris followed them, throwing taunting remarks at Nita, until they were locked into the cell tier. This time they were both put into one cell, and Nita was thankful for that, since it gave her an opportunity to comfort the child.

She fondled the fiery red head of Elaine Robillard, in her lap, and glanced up as the corridor door opened. Her eyes widened in consternation as she saw the short, stumpy, waddling figure of the cripple, Chenab Sind, enter the corridor, followed by a half-naked, hooded leper, with the symbol of the cobra painted on his chest. Then Chenab Sind had betrayed them. He was in league with Tang-akhmut—what else was he doing here?

Nita crouched in the shadow of the cell, and allowed the two to go through without seeing her. As the hooded man passed the cell, she felt an unaccountable rush of blood to her temples, as if there were some strange sort of affinity between them. But she crouched there, silent, until they had disappeared through the other door on the way to the audience room.

She could not understand that sudden feeling that had coursed through her at the approach of the hooded man. Why should she be affected by one who was repulsive? But was he repulsive? She found her eyes straying after him. There had been something vaguely familiar about that hooded man's walk, about the way he carried himself—something she should have recognized. Suddenly there was a catch in her throat, and a cry died on her lips.

That man was Richard Wentworth! She knew it, was sure of it, would have staked her life on it!

Trembling, she disengaged herself from Elaine, who raised her head. "What is it, Nita?" the child asked.

"S-sh!" Nita left her there, went close to the grilled door, tried to peer down the corridor. Though the far door had been left open, she could not see either the cripple or the hooded man.

They had passed through the next room, which was where the gas tanks and gas masks were stored. Nita leaned against the door in an effort to see further, and suddenly *the door gave!*

She understood then that the hooded man had slipped the catch of the lock as he went past behind Chenab Sind. What further proof was needed that he was Richard Wentworth! Still trembling, she called softly to Elaine, pushed the door wide open and stepped out into the corridor.

IN THE meantime, Chenab Sind, with Wentworth behind him, had entered the audience room. Tang-akhmut set upon his dais, in low-voiced conversation with Vara Kun and Yahatma. There were half a dozen of the Hindus present, but Issoris had gone into another part of the building.

Tang-akhmut looked up as Chenab Sind entered, and glared at the hooded man behind the cripple. He said sternly: "You know, Chenab Sind, that no lepers are allowed here. Why did you bring this one?"

Wentworth, unarmed, stood directly behind the cripple. He had doubted Chenab Sind's story from the first, but he had allowed himself to be led in here. Now, from the way Tang-akhmut spoke to the legless man, Wentworth understood that the cripple's story had been a fabrication from the first. He understood that the attack upon Chenab Sind at Nita's house had been nothing but an elaborate build-up to ingratiate the cripple into his confidence. All that flashed through his mind in a split second, and was immediately confirmed by Chenab Sind himself, who leaped nimbly to one side on his stumps of legs, and snouted: "This is Wentworth! Seize him!"

Even then, Wentworth might not have been sure of Chenab Sind's treachery. The cripple certainly had not intended for him to learn of it until he was actually out of Wentworth's reach. He had therefore shouted his warning in Hindustani, forgetting that Wentworth's servant was a Sikh; forgetting that Wentworth had practiced Hindustani with Ram Singh for many a weary hour, and that he understood it as well as anyone in that room.

So, as the meaning of the cripple's shout registered with him, Wentworth's mind and body coördinated in a lightning movement that took everyone in the room by surprise.

Vara Kun and Yahatma were already leaping across the room toward him, knives in hand, and the other Hindus were closing in. Wentworth reached down and seized the cripple by his one arm, clamping the wrist tight.

Then, as the knife men rushed, he raised Chenab Sind from the floor as if he had been a child, swung him up, *and hurled him straight at Yahatma, who was closest.*

The legless man screeched horribly as he hurtled through the air. His deformed body struck Yahatma full in the face, and the two of them smashed into the dais where Tang-akhmut stood.

The others had stopped for an instant as the cripple's body became a human catapult, and in that instant Wentworth leaped backward out of the room. He bumped into some one, whirled, and uttered a glad cry as he recognized Nita.

Nita exclaimed: "These tanks, Dick! Our only chance. They're full of gas!"

She thrust a mask at him, and he saw that the little girl who stood beside her already had a mask on, and that Nita was also donning one.

Vara Kun had already reached the doorway, and the coiled cobra around the snake-charmer's neck was licking out toward Wentworth. The Hindus were crowding in alongside Vara Kun, filling the doorway. And Wentworth smashed at faces with the gas mask Nita had handed him, catching knife thrusts with it, keeping the murderous throng from pushing through the doorway. For a moment he thrust them back, and Nita, just behind him, slammed the door.

Wentworth leaned against it while Nita and little Elaine wrestled with the nozzle of one of the tanks, playing with a valve. Wentworth ripped off his rubber mask, and slipped on the gas mask just as a mighty heave from the other side caused the door to give. Nita had the nozzle ready, and nodded to him. He leaped away from the door and it gave, piling Vara Kun and the Hindus on the floor.

NITA TURNED the valve, and a thick, cloudy gas hissed out of the tank. Vara Kun saw it, screeched, and scrambled back into the audience room, with the Hindus behind. But the gas was too volatile, had been planned too murderously. It caught them before they had taken three steps. They doubled over, shrieking in agony.

At the far side of the room Wentworth saw Tang-akhmut running toward a door at the left of the dais. The Princess Issoris had appeared in the room from another entrance, and she had seen the gas, was turning back to escape through the same way she had come. And the gas caught them both in the act of escaping. Wentworth turned away, blocking Nita's view of the hideous sight of those people dying in the agony they had planned for others.

The three of them made their way back through the cell corridor, into the room where Nita had seen the lepers. She closed her eyes, and swayed, would have fallen had not Wentworth supported her. The gas had preceded them here. The sight made her sick. Elaine clung close to her as Wentworth helped them through.

There was another room to the left, and an open safe, which had probably been the precinct safe at one time. In front of the safe one of the Hindus lay dead, from the gas. Wentworth stepped over his body, fingered through papers and ledgers. One of them he raised triumphantly, showed it to Nita. Its title page bore the inscription:

Record of the Deeds of the Living Pharaoh in New York

There was a page marked: "How the Living Pharaoh laid murder at the door of his enemies." It was a complete account of the way Wentworth and Kirkpatrick had been framed for murder. It would clear them completely!

Tang-akhmut's inordinate vanity had caused him to leave a record which would serve his enemy!

Wentworth handed the book to Nita, who had recovered somewhat, and rummaged further in the safe. On the floor lay a hypodermic needle marked: "Leprosy infection." It had apparently been dropped by the man who lay there dead. He must have been getting it for use upon Nita and Elaine. Wentworth passed this up, and examined a row of vials in a rack. These were all neatly marked in Arabic, which he read clearly: "Private formula of Chenab Sind for the cure of leprosy."

He stuffed these in his trouser pockets, eagerly; they would afford relief to the women who had been infected at Fremont and Tynan's. He had found what he sought!

Only then was he ready to leave the, gas-filled building. He piloted Nita and Elaine out into the open air, where they went a good distance down the road before ripping off the masks.

The three of them stood looking solemnly at each other, forgetful of the autos that honked at them, forgetful of the crowd that gathered to stare at Wentworth's naked torso with the symbol of the cobra.

At last he said to Nita, almost in a whisper: "At last, dear, the end of Tang-akhmut!"

Nita shivered, closed her eyes. "It—it was like a nightmare!"

"But that's all over now," he said. "Richard Wentworth and Nita van Sloan are going on a long vacation, away from this city—just the two of us—"

"No, darling," she corrected. "Just the three of us." She pressed Elaine Robillard's head tight against her breast.

Printed in Great Britain
by Amazon